"I told you what I came for," he said

He reached out a hand to pin her gently against the door as she tried to sidestep him.

Her heart jumped into her throat and her limbs started to tremble. She licked her lips and stared up into his face, so close to her own now, and felt as if she were drowning in his somber, heavy-lidded gaze. He brought his other hand up and traced the outline of her lips with one finger.

"Do you know what your mouth reminds me of, Morgan?" he asked. "It's like some ripe beautiful fruit ready to be savored."

He lowered his head and his mouth descended on hers. Morgan found that she didn't have the will to resist, didn't have the will to do anything but revel in the unfamiliar sensations of her body.

LINDSAY ARMSTRONG

melt a frozen heart

Harlequin Books

TORONTO • NEW YORK • LOS ANGELES • LONDON
AMSTERDAM • PARIS • SYDNEY • HAMBURG
STOCKHOLM • ATHENS • TOKYO • MILAN

Harlequin Presents first edition January 1983
ISBN 0-373-10559-2

Original hardcover edition published in 1982
by Mills & Boon Limited

CHAPTER ONE

THE girl behind the desk fingered several multi-coloured brochures and eyed them with a tinge of envy. For they depicted golden bodies draped on pale beaches that were lapped by azure waters and fringed by coconut palms—a sight for sore eyes as the first chill fingers of winter made themselves felt in this southern corner of Queensland.

Indeed, to the elderly couple who had just vacated the comfortably upholstered swivel chairs on the other side of the desk, the glossy scenes had been sufficiently riveting to cause them to arrange to pay several thousand dollars of their life's savings on a package tour to Fiji.

The girl behind the desk smiled faintly. Her clients had candidly admitted that they'd never been farther afield from Brisbane than Toowoomba, a distance of about seventy miles, and she couldn't help wondering just how they'd cope with the jet-setting milieu they were due to enter shortly on their cherished, once-in-a-lifetime, 'real' vacation.

'Of course we've been to Bribie Island and the Gold Coast,' the old man had admitted, and added with engaging frankness, 'but we're determined to see something of the world before we die!'

And going to see it they were. In style, too. Their part cruise-part air tour included visits to Auckland, Suva, Noumea, Pago Pago and Rabaul—all places that fired the imagination but could be a little rough on staid, elderly digestive systems, if not downright exhausting to the physique.

'I hope they have fun, though,' the girl murmured to herself, still with a faraway look in her hazel eyes, and then with a tiny shrug, she scooped the brochures into an envelope file and snapped it shut with a flick of her long, exquisitely manicured fingers. She fiddled for a moment with the unusual gold ring on the little finger of her left hand and pursed her lips thoughtfully.

Let's see, she thought, what's next? I must issue the Sandersons' air-tickets today and I promised Mr Wallace a quotation on his horribly complicated flying tour of Europe, although I know he'll change his mind six times before we finally get to the reservation stage. And argue with me about how we could make it cheaper! I really don't know why he doesn't set up his own travel agency with himself as chief fare consultant.

She glanced across at the vacant desk beside her own in the plush, brightly decorated office and then checked her watch. It appeared her colleague, Ryan Clarke, was having an extended lunch—yet again, she thought with a wry look.

'Probably chatting up some bird,' she added to herself sotto-voce in an imitation of her colleague's phraseology. Ryan was a good-looking bright young man, but it couldn't be denied that he saved his best energies for the pursuit of what he called the 'perfect female'. Nor could it be denied that he was an incurable optimist.

'But he's met his match so far as I'm concerned,' the girl muttered as her thoughts turned to words. 'I like him—you can't help it somehow, but I've no intention of being chatted up like the rest of them! Surely he must know that by now?'

She laughed at herself then, slightly ruefully. Because Ryan Clarke was still laying determined siege to her, in between other affairs, although they'd been working together for nearly a year now and despite innumerable heavy snubs on her part.

She gathered the file and stood up, still smiling wryly. She crossed to a filing cabinet and replaced the file and then stood poised, wondering whether to start issuing air tickets for the Sanderson family or to get stuck into Mr Wallace's fare quotation.

She sighed faintly and brought her hands up to run them through long shining chestnut hair that was cut in a fringe across her wide forehead and curved slightly beneath her chin like a rounded curtain of chestnut silk framing her perfectly oval face with its delicately cut mouth, straight little nose and hazel eyes that looked green in some lights.

She flicked her fringe sideways and rested her hands on her hips as she pondered. She was a girl of about medium height and the uniform provided by the travel agency did justice to her slim figure—a well-fitting white blouse that emphasised her bosom beneath its prim pintucking and her tiny waist where the blouse met the top of her straight navy-blue skirt and the slender sweep of her legs below the skirt, impeccably encased in pale tights and her feet in elegantly high, navy-blue leather shoes.

But it wasn't just her face and her figure that made this girl stand out anywhere. It was her perfect grooming too, and the graceful way she moved and used her hands.

She came to a decision and pulled open a drawer. The narrow gold bangle on her right wrist clattered faintly against it. But she hesitated with her fingers on the airline tickets in the drawer and then suddenly, as she was overwhelmed by some curious sixth sense, she turned to her desk and gave a tiny gasp.

Someone had come in without her being aware of it.

'Oh! You gave me a start. I didn't hear you! I . . .' Her warm, greeting-the-clients smile faded and her eyes widened as she took in the tall untidy figure standing between her desk and the entrance.

She groped for the back of her chair and moistened her lips, because across the office stood the one man she had devoutly hoped she would never see again. Ever.

'Well, if it isn't little Glamorgan Jones!' the man said

with quizzically raised brows and he dropped his tattered duffel bag to the floor and cast himself down in a chair. He studied her critically as she stood with a hand to her mouth in a pose of frozen embarrassment. 'You know, you've blossomed almost unbelievably,' he said with his blue eyes bright and appreciative.

Morgan came to life then and sat down herself. 'Life's full of surprises, isn't it?' she returned with a sweetness she was far from feeling as a faint tinge of colour stained her pale skin. 'You haven't changed.'

He grimaced and drew a hand through his bushy fair hair. 'Thank you,' he said politely. 'Do you mean physically or otherwise?' he added with a look of mock concern. 'I seem to recall that on the last occasion we met, you thought I was the most insufferable creature you'd ever come across.'

'I mean physically,' she said coolly. 'How could I know if you'd changed any other way?'

'How indeed?' he agreed. 'But then I was never too sure whether the insufferable tag you labelled me with was reserved for my personality or . . . both. You did tell me the very sight of me made you sick. That's if I recall correctly?' He put his head on one side and regarded her amusedly.

She gritted her teeth and called on every ounce of her hard-won poise. 'I was a little . . . distraught at the time,' she said mildly. 'I probably said a few silly things. Anyway,' she added brightly, 'what can I do for you? Are you off to the Himalayas or the depths of Papua New Guinea?'

He narrowed his eyes faintly and ignored her question completely. 'Did you get your degree, Glamorgan?'

'No, I didn't,' she said steadily enough, although her fingernails were biting into her palms. 'And please don't call me that. I'm plainly and simply Morgan Jones now, and that's how I prefer to be addressed.'

He grinned. 'Simply Morgan Jones—that I accept. Plain Morgan Jones?—there I'm forced to quibble. There's nothing plain about you any more, honey. You're gorgeous. But I suppose when I say that, I'm joining a long queue. Tell me,' he rested a hand idly about his ankle which was reposing on his other knee and exhibiting a rather batted sand-shoe, 'what brought about this stunning metamorphosis? I'm really interested.'

Morgan gritted her teeth again and felt a little flame of anger lick through her. There could be no doubting that he was as interested as he said. His intelligent, deep blue eyes were fairly sparking with interest. The same kind of interest she'd seen him long ago display towards a piece of dolomite or any other kind of rock. The same vital, vivid kind of interest that had led her into a terrible trap ... unwittingly on his part, she always admitted to herself. Grudgingly. ...

But I shall never be so badly misled again, she thought mutinously. And I'm not going to be treated like an interesting clinical study either!

She said stiffly, 'I'm sorry, but I'm really rather busy.' She flashed an indignant glance towards Ryan's still empty desk. How come he was never there when she needed him but always underfoot at other times? At least he could have provided her with some moral support.

She picked up her pen. 'What can I arrange for you?' she asked seriously.

'Oh, nothing! I'm not going anywhere at the moment. Matter of fact, I've just come back.'

'Well, why did you come in here, then?' Morgan asked with a trace of impatience.

'Because my bus-stop happens to be right outside,' he said obligingly. 'And while I was out there killing time, I was gazing at your exotic posters when it suddenly dawned on me that the sheila behind the desk reminded me of someone I knew, so I came in to investigate.' He shrugged. 'I was right. Will you have lunch with me, Gl ... er ... Morgan?'

'No, thank you. I'm afraid I shall be working right through my lunch hour today.'

'I see,' he said gravely but with his eyes laughing at her.

She stirred restlessly as Ryan rushed through the doorway and plonked himself down at his desk. But the man in front of her didn't give him more than an uninterested glance.

Instead he said to her, 'Do you have a car, Morgan?'

She hesitated, slightly bewildered. 'I ... yes. Why do you ask?' She was immediately conscious that Ryan had pricked his ears.

'Well, I'm between cars at the moment. I thought I could hitch a ride home with you to my place tonight and in exchange, feed you. What time do you close?'

Morgan opened and closed her mouth several times but could get no words out, and it was Ryan who said politely, 'Five o'clock.'

'Good.' The man on the other side of the desk stood up. 'I'll meet you outside on the dot. See you later, Morgan. You too, Mr ... Clarke,' he added as Ryan moved a stack of papers from in front of his name plaque. He heaved his duffel bag on to his shoulder and sauntered out.

'Wait ... hang on!' Morgan called desperately, and tripped over her waste-paper basket as she tried to run after him. But her headlong flight was further impeded by the arrival into the office at that moment of Mr Wallace, who bore down upon her with an expression of gleeful anticipation.

'Miss Jones! Have you started on that fare yet? I've one or two little changes to make. . . .' He turned then to see what was fixing Morgan's attention so avidly over his right shoulder, but all he could see was a tall man with a duffel bag boarding a bus. 'Miss Jones?' he said tentatively.

'Yes, Mr Wallace—I mean no.' Morgan turned back to her desk and ignored Ryan's lascivious wink. 'I haven't started yet. How many changes did you have in mind?' she asked, and nobly withheld any trace of long-suffering from her voice and countenance.

It was at least an hour later, during which Ryan had obviously been bursting with curiosity, that there was a sufficient lull for him to say, 'Now come on, Morgan, spill the beans to Uncle Ryan. Who was that man? And don't look blank, I mean the one who wants to hijack you off to dinner at his pad tonight. The only man,' he added truculently, 'I've ever seen you with who wasn't a business associate or a client. You do realise I'm devastated, don't you? And liable to fade away from a broken heart?'

'No, you're not!' she said tartly, and then had to relent at his mournful expression. 'Oh, you are an idiot, Ryan,' she said with a giggle.

'I'm still waiting. Who is he?'

'He's. . . .' She sighed. 'Well, he was one of my lecturers at university,' she said baldly.

'I thought so!'

'Now how could you possibly have thought anything of the kind?' she demanded. 'He was wearing faded old jeans, running shoes and he had a tear in his shirt. Are you trying to tell me you're a clairvoyant?'

'Not at all,' Ryan said blandly. He eyed her irate expression. 'Don't take on so,' he drawled. 'All I was going to say was that it was obvious he was no conventional hippie. The man had an aura, sweetheart, and it doesn't surprise me to hear that he's a lecturer at all. But I can't help wondering why you're so hot under the collar,' he added meekly yet with a keen twinkle in his eye.

Morgan drew a deep breath and counted to ten. 'I am not,' she said firmly. 'Besides, I thought hippies by definition were supremely unconventional.'

'Which just goes to show that you're a little behind the times, Morgan,' he said patronisingly. 'I did suspect it.'

'Only because I wouldn't hop into bed with you after our first introduction,' she retorted acidly.

'Have you ever been to bed with him—our lecturer mate?' Ryan asked with quizzically raised eyebrows.

'I have not,' she said flatly. 'And it's none of your business anyway. Don't you *ever* think about anything else?'

He looked her up and down and said with a grin, 'Believe me, Morgan, you make it very difficult. You turn my working hours into a nightmare of frustration!'

She shut her eyes and turned away deliberately, and stoically refused to talk to him for a good ten minutes until he said finally in a laughing plea, 'Okay! Okay! I won't mention it again, today anyway. But I'm really interested in this character, your unconventional hippie. Are you going to have dinner with him? Do you think it's wise?'

'What do you mean?' she asked quickly.

'Listen, honey . . . you know I really get worried about you sometimes!' he said exasperatedly. 'It was obvious to me, in about two minutes flat, mind, that the man had a whole lot going for him, and the fact he gets around in old clothes didn't hide it. Incidentally, *that*'s what I meant when I said you were behind the times. A whole lot of stuffy conventions about dress and so on have gone by the board these days. And blue jeans in fact are more a status symbol these days than an instant identification tag to being down and out and having to resort to hippiedom!'

She stared at him and had to smile faintly, not only at his terminology but his passionate delivery. 'Go on,' she said. 'I'm listening.'

'I hope you're learning too! And the other thing about this man,' he went on with a suddenly rueful inflection, 'is that I have no doubt that he has sheilas lying down in the aisles for him. That kind of controlled power and those faintly off-beat looks generally do—in my experience, anyway. So I'd watch your step if I were you, Morgan sweetheart. You might just have met your match. And not before time, might I add!'

She felt a little trickle of guilt then at his words. She said uncertainly, 'I'm sorry, Ryan. I know you think I'm the original prude, but it's not that I feel I'm above you or anyone else, at all. I just . . . well, if I sounded that way, I didn't mean to.'

'I know that,' he said with a rare gravity. 'I also know something pretty painful must have made you the way you are. No,' he shook his head, as she stirred restlessly, 'I don't want to probe. But I'm very fond of you, Morgan, as a friend, as one of the most kindhearted girls I've ever met, and I'd only like to see you happy—really happy, I mean.'

The little silence that greeted his words stretched. Morgan stared at her fingers unseeingly and marvelled at this side of Ryan, a side she'd never even suspected. And a feeling of warmth touched her heart.

He leant over and patted her shoulder. 'My,' he said flippantly, 'all this emotion! But to get back to my original question?'

'. . . Is it wise to have dinner with him?' Morgan said slowly. 'It's not really a question of that. He may be a lady-killer, but this is one lady he's immune to. The thing is I don't . . . I mean. . . .'

'Well then, I'd say go!' Ryan was emphatic. 'If you're not worried about being dined and wined and *seduced*— why not? That's just what you need. To get out and meet different people, renew old acquaintances, broaden your outlook. I'm sure he wouldn't be dull and boring, now would he?'

Morgan compressed her lips. 'Ryan, I'm glad you like me as a friend and I like you very much too, but *I'll* choose who I go out to dinner with, thank you very much!'

'Ah. I see. Despite your brave words you are scared of him, aren't you, Morgan?'

She set her teeth. 'You're impossible, you know. . . .' She stopped with her hand raised. 'But you are still my junior, Ryan Clarke, and as such it will be very good experience for you to try and work out this fare.' She tossed a piece of paper on to his desk. 'Now remember what I've taught you about open jaw fares, dog-legs and so on.'

'Morgan!' he protested indignantly. 'Not old Wallace's meanderings?'

'The same,' she said deliberately. 'You'll note that he's starting off from Brisbane but he's returning to Perth. Apparently he's had a lifelong ambition to cross the Nullabor by train—the Indian Pacific, so that complicates it a little.'

'A little!' Ryan moaned. 'You're a heartless, ungrateful. . . .'

At five to five Morgan looked up at a nudge from Ryan.

'You better think fast, because your ex-lecturer is a-crossin' the street! Decided how you're going to say no to him? What's his name, by the way?' he asked.

'Steven Harrow,' she replied tartly, and coloured faintly. She looked round a little desperately as if to judge the avenues of escape open to her as the man on the pavement lowered his duffel bag to the ground right beside the entrance and waved to her through the glass. Then he turned away to contemplate the traffic with his arms folded and shoulders resting negligently against the glass.

'The nerve of him!' Morgan stuttered. She turned on Ryan, who was laughing heartily. 'You too!' she spat at him. 'Well, I'll just show you that I'm not afraid of him or you or anyone else!' She tossed her head and her hair flew out like a silken waterfall under the neon lighting.

'Do you mean you're going to go?' Ryan asked incredulously, but still trying to smother his laughter.

'Yes! And what's more, I shall be in full command of this evening; and if he doesn't like it, then I shall be able to say, I told you so!'

'Wow!' Ryan ducked playfully. 'Maybe I should go out and warn him? Tell him to take out another insurance policy . . . all right, all right! I won't say another word.'

'You'd better not,' she said grimly as she gathered up her bag and jacket and tidied her desk. 'And you may have the pleasure of locking up—when you've completed that fare quotation. And don't you dare be late tomorrow morning!'

'No, miss,' he said meekly. 'Do you like apples, miss?'

Morgan took a deep breath and turned away deliberately. She stalked to the door without a backward glance and luckily missed the very real glint of admiration that was mingled with laughter in Ryan's eyes.

'Hell,' he said softly as the front door of the office closed decisively behind Morgan. 'What a figure, what a face—and what a temper! Man, what I wouldn't give to be the one who brings her to heel!'

Morgan's shiny yellow Mini seemed curiously to have shrunk. She noted this with a wry glance at her passenger, who was having some trouble disposing of his lengthy frame in comfort.

'Do you live far out of town?' she asked idly as she drove steadily and carefully through the heavy traffic.

'Not really,' Steve Harrow said. 'Once you get on to Waterworks Road just keep going. Er . . . there's a rather large semi-trailer breathing down our neck,' he added with his head turned to the rear. 'Er . . . I'm not even sure that you're in his line of visibility, so I wouldn't do anything unexpected.'

Morgan gritted her teeth and at the first opportunity turned into the kerb and brought the little car to a halt.

He looked at her expectantly. 'Would you like me to drive?' he offered.

'No. No, I would not,' she said sweetly. 'I'd just like to remind you that this is my car and that I'm a licensed driver. If you have any criticisms, you have only to open that door and get out. I won't be particularly devastated, not only if I don't have dinner with you tonight, but for that matter, if I never see you again. And perhaps I could even offer you some advice? If you have such an aversion to little cars and women drivers, it might be an idea if you get yourself a car.'

His face was alive with amusement as she stopped speaking. 'Bravo!' he said. 'That puts me in my place well and truly. You've changed, Morgan, in more ways than one. But thank you, no, I shall not alight. In fact I feel suitably chastened and shall utter nothing further that could be construed as criticism.'

'I'm so glad,' she said politely, and put the car into gear although she would have dearly loved to slap his face. Really I do hate men, she thought irately as she ducked expertly into the stream of traffic once more. They're so unbelievably conceited and superior!

Their conversation from then on was desultory and mainly confined to problems Brisbane was suffering as its main arterial roads suffered an ever-increasing build-up of traffic.

Until Morgan said finally, 'I knew Waterworks Road was long, but does it ever end?' She pulled up at yet another red traffic light and shielded her eyes from the setting sun.

'It's not that far now,' said Steve.

'Neither are Mount Glorious or Mount Nebo,' she pointed out, referring to the hilly wooded area on Brisbane's eastern extremity.

'That's what I mean.'

She drew a breath. 'Is that where you live? Why didn't you say so before?' she demanded.

'Well, I thought you might not come, you see. Seeing that I couldn't offer you transport myself.'

'You thought right,' she said flatly. 'But if you haven't got a car, how on earth do you get to and fro yourself?'

'I take the bus as far as The Gap and then I hitch a ride. I've never yet had to walk the full way.'

'Oh. Why?'

'Why don't I have a car? I made a pact with myself that I wouldn't own one for twelve months. My . . . er . . . contribution to the so-called fuel crisis. Also—that's my bus you're passing now, by the way,' he said as she skirted an orange and white Council bus, 'at least, the one I would have been on, if I hadn't met you today. Er . . . what was I saying? Oh yes, when you feel you're becoming totally dependent on something, like cars, I often think it's wise to cut the association before it becomes an addiction.'

She said with a lifted eyebrow, 'But you haven't forsworn them completely? You don't mind accepting lifts?'

'Not at all,' he said airily. 'That would be like cutting off your nose to spite your face.'

'How very convenient,' she commented. 'Your philosophy, I mean.'

He shot her a keen glance and raised an eyebrow. 'Do I detect a note of sarcasm?' he queried.

'Yes, you do.'

He reached out and touched her hair. 'You're very cynical, Glamorgan,' he said softly. 'I had hoped you'd mend a little better.'

Morgan laughed coldly and moved her head. 'When? When did you think about me long enough to hope or even wonder?'

'You'd be surprised,' he said softly. 'I rather had you on my conscience.'

She closed her eyes briefly. That makes me feel just great, she thought drearily. Just great.

'You mean ... you knew?' she asked in a cracked voice.

'It was difficult not to. How is your father ... no, don't tell me yet. Wait until we get home. It's not far now—really.'

CHAPTER TWO

THE view from Steven Harrow's tree-house—for that was what it reminded Morgan of—was fantastic, even as the light faded and Moreton Bay with its attendant islands of Moreton and Stradbroke dimmed and disappeared beyond the tall spires of Brisbane city and a myriad little lights sprang up to prick the velvety dusk.

She was out on the wood deck that served as a terrace, nursing a drink, having been firmly banished from the kitchen.

'You did the chauffeuring, I'll do the cooking,' Steve had said with wave of his hand. 'Besides, I don't like people watching me cook. It makes me nervous. Take your drink outside and soak up the view.'

Morgan had obeyed and even found herself relaxing a little as the sun set and some delicious mouthwatering aromas issued from the kitchen.

And presently, when it was quite dark, she stirred and walked back inside. 'Can I look around your house?' she called.

'Sure,' came his somewhat muffled reply.

It was a small house, perched as it was, rather precariously she thought, on the hillside and surrounded by tall gum trees. Perhaps because it was built entirely of beautifully seasoned mellow wood inside and out, it gave the 'tree-house' impression, she mused idly as she wandered around. But although the furnishing was sparse, it was also quite exquisite and not the normal boxwood variety she dimly remembered from her childhood days when she had shared a tree-house with the little boy next door.

The lounge-dining room quite frankly enchanted her, with its enormous padded and buttoned leather settee in a rich brown, two winged armchairs covered in pale aquamarine velvet and carpeted with a fine close-pile, pure wool carpet in oyster beige. The small dining-room table was a solid sheet of glass supported by gleaming chrome tubular legs and the chairs were also of tubular chrome with wicker backs and seats enamelled to match the aquamarine chairs.

A wicker-work chest-type low table with brass handles stood between the settee and the chairs and in one corner a basket container sprouted a dozen or so tall, feathery pampas grass plumes, their silky heads coloured silver and pale gold in the lamplight flanking a fireplace.

Between the lounge and the wooden deck was one whole wall of louvred folding doors instead of the conventional glass sliding doors and a roll-down filigree bamboo blind instead of curtains. A good idea, she thought. Cool and possibly mosquito-proof at the same time.

She wandered down a short passageway and into one of the only other two rooms in the house apart from the kitchen.

This room was a bedroom and again supremely uncluttered. In fact there was only a huge bed which bore signs beneath its rich, ruby-red velvet cover of having been rather hastily made; and one cabinet beside it supporting a lamp with a silk lampshade of the same colour as the bedspread. The oyster carpet was repeated in here too, and the two splashes of vivid ruby-red were quite breathtakingly luxurious against the warm brown of the wooden walls.

Morgan peeped through an archway that led off the bedroom, to see that it opened into a small dressing room beyond which she glimpsed a royal-blue tiled bathroom with gold fittings.

Her eyes widened slightly. For a man who didn't own

a car, he didn't believe in skimping on other luxuries, she thought a trifle sardonically.

The last room wasn't quite in keeping with the rest of the house, however. It too opened on to the deck as did the bedroom, by way of the same folding louvred doors, but there was no carpeting on the floor, no rich use of colours. Simply a large desk sporting a typewriter and an incredible litter of papers and one whole wall of book-shelving. And one chair.

So that's what he's doing stuck out here in the bush, she thought. Writing another book. I wonder what this one's about? Another geography textbook?

She turned and jumped, for her host was standing right behind her.

'I didn't hear you!'

'That's the second time today,' Steve commented wryly. 'Dinner is served, ma'am.' He stood aside and allowed her to precede him into the lounge.

'Dinner' was a simple meal—thick juicy slices of steak served with a crisp salad and an interesting side dish which he obligingly identified for her as zucchini lightly sautéed and combined with onion and tomato also sautéed and then covered with grated cheese and breadcrumbs and slipped under the grill until golden and melted.

'A pinch of fresh black pepper too,' he added. 'Like it?'

'Mmm! It's delicious. Did you whip this all up . . . now, since we've been here?'

'Not the zucchini. I made that this morning. All I had to do was put it under the grill.'

'You're talented,' she said idly as she sipped her wine. She studied him covertly as they ate.

It was true that he'd changed little in the last five years. He still had that broad-shouldered, narrow-hipped and elegantly streamlined body that had played havoc with her naïve eighteen-year-old heart . . . was it only five years ago since that final, traumatic encounter? she asked herself. It felt more like ten.

Yes, and as Ryan had so accurately described it, his slightly off-beat brand of looks had weathered particularly well, and she felt almost as if she was being transported back in time as she eyed his tanned face with its strong lines, his white teeth and blue eyes that could be be so uncomfortably piercing at times, his bushy fair hair . . . perhaps some new fine lines that crinkled around his eyes when he smiled, she mused. But apart from that, at thirty-five, as she knew him to be, he really looked no different from when he'd been thirty.

It's not *really* fair, she thought with a tiny pang. I wish he'd developed a paunch or gone bald! Ah, but Morgan, she chided herself, although he might not have changed, you have. You've proved yourself since those days.

He broke in upon her reflections by saying, 'Well, tell me what you've been doing with yourself since we last met, Glamorgan.' He removed her plate and topped up her wine-glass. 'I'm afraid it's only fruit for dessert—perhaps a little later?'

'Whatever you like. Your dinner was delicious,' she said with a glinting smile. 'Quite ample reward for my chauffeuring services.'

He grinned wryly and lay back in his chair, holding his wine-glass to the light as he twirled it slowly. 'I'm listening,' he said after a long moment.

Morgan raised her eyebrows. 'I've got a better idea,' she offered. 'Why don't you tell me what you've been doing with yourself since we last met? I'm sure it's much more interesting.'

He regarded her thoughtfully, but she stared back at him unflinchingly. 'I see,' he said at last, and then, 'All right. I've,' he ticked off his lean powerful fingers, 'spent some time at Oxford on an exchange fellowship, I had a year's sabbatical in the Middle East, then I came back to Griffith for a while and built this house in my spare time.

What else? Oh yes, I joined an expedition for a few months trying to track Torres' path around Cape York through the Straits named after him. I really enjoyed that until we got caught in a cyclone and lost our boat. Er . . . and I spent some time on Mornington Island in the Gulf of Carpentaria.'

'Studying the local land formations?' she queried.

'Not really—well, I didn't precisely ignore them but I've gone into a new field now. I'm writing a thesis for a Master's in Anthropology.'

'Oh?' she said, her interest genuinely caught for a moment. 'Why the change? I thought you were such a dedicated geographer!'

'I guess I'll always be that, but Anthropology in a way is quite related, so it's not a total departure. And I find it fascinating.'

'And in the midst of all this activity, you've had time for women?' she asked.

'I wouldn't say that precisely,' he answered with an amused flash of his blue, blue eyes. 'But if you're delicately trying to discover whether I have a wife, no, I don't.'

Morgan shrugged. 'I did wonder.' She looked around her.

'Oh.' Steve laughed then. 'You're referring to the decor? No, that's all my own idea. Do you like it?'

'I do.'

'I'm glad. Women on the whole do seem to approve of it,' he said lazily. 'One of your fair sisters even told me I should go into interior decorating.'

'Did she really,' Morgan said casually. 'Was she your mistress?'

He put his wine-glass down slowly and folded his arms across his chest. 'Mistress, lover,' he shrugged. 'Call it what you like.' He contemplated his glass for a moment and then his long, gold-tipped lashes swept up and he let his blue gaze play over her thoughtfully. 'Why the interest, Glamorgan? I must say I find it a bit surprising.'

'Please don't call me that,' she said evenly. 'And I don't know why you should be surprised. I'm pretty sure you were going to ask me the same kind of questions. Most men do after they've wined and dined you. But isn't there an old saying about the goose and the gander?' she queried gently.

He narrowed his eyes, but his expression was quite unreadable and it was only when she noticed a muscle jerk once in his jaw that she knew she had angered him.

Good, she thought acidly with a tinge of triumph. Now perhaps he'll realise that I'm not prepared to be dissected by anyone, least of all him.

She stood up and gathered the plates. 'Will you let me make the coffee?' she asked conversationally. 'I don't feel like anything else, and besides, I ought to get going fairly soon . . .' Her words were cut off by a sharp gasp as his hand shot out and closed painfully around her wrist.

She tried to pull back and glared at him furiously. 'Just what do you think you're doing?' she demanded fiercely through her teeth.

'This,' he said flatly, and stood up himself in one fluid movement and drew her into the middle of the room.

She reacted wildly, trying to claw him with her nails and pull herself from his grasp, but he was far too strong for her and he captured her other wrist in his hand with little effort.

'And this,' he said implacably as he undid the buttons of her prim white blouse and pushed it off her shoulders together with her bra straps so that the ivory skin of her breasts was exposed.

'And this,' he said again as he flicked his hand through her hair, disordering its smooth gleaming sweep.

Morgan cried out inarticulately, a desperate wordless plea, but it only made him tighten his grasp of a handful of hair and pull her head back before his lips came down punishingly and bruisingly on her own.

She couldn't speak when he raised his head at last and released her wrists. Instead she swayed slightly and raised trembling fingers to her swollen mouth, and had not the strength or the will to resist when he picked her up and sat her in one of the velvet chairs.

'There,' he said as he stood looking down at her, his face grim but his eyes curiously concerned. 'It's out in the open now, isn't it, Morgan? With a few variations that's how you looked when I stumbled over you in the campus grounds on that last night—when those two inebriated young hooligans you were with took fright and bolted after coming so close to raping you. Do you think I don't know or can't see that you'd rather run under a bus than be in the same room with me? Do you think I can't guess the humiliation the sight of me makes you feel? But I won't allow you to go on burying it, Morgan, like a festering wound. And I'm not prepared to skirt around it either. You've grown a bright, brittle protective covering which doesn't amuse me and doesn't suit you. And we're going to start exorcising all the ghosts and painful memories right here tonight.'

He turned on his heel and splashed some brandy from a crystal decanter into a glass.

'Here, drink this,' he said entirely impersonally.

Morgan took the glass with a shaking hand and sipped the brandy feeling its warmth slide down her throat. Then with fumbling fingers she did up her blouse, not able to lift her eyes to his, and felt herself colour faintly.

Oh God, I hate him, she thought. How could he have done it like this? How?

He drew up the other armchair and leant across to tilt her chin upwards with gentle fingers. 'Look at me, Morgan.'

She did then, unable to hide the blaze of anger and pain in her eyes.

He said roughly, 'The surgeon's knife isn't painless, Morgan, but it's the only way.'

'Is it?' she whispered. 'There is ... *was* another way. All you had to do was turn away from that window today. That would have been just as effective.'

'No, it wouldn't,' he said steadily. 'I turned my back on you once. I thought then it was the best way, but I was wrong. I don't intend to be wrong again. You see, yes, I did know you had that crush on me—I'd known for some time. But it's an occupational hazard when you're teaching impressionable young girls, and if you have any integrity, you learn to deal with it.'

Oh God, I could die, Morgan thought miserably.

'My method,' Steve went on, 'was to ignore it, and you'd be amazed how many times that succeeded. But what I didn't know, until I took you home that night, was your family background. Your father. And I didn't know until some time later that you'd been goaded into undesirable company by a mixture of his repressive nature and some unkind classmate's taunts about how you were going around with your heart on sleeve over your geography lecturer.'

Morgan wiped away a tear. 'It wasn't your problem then and it isn't now,' she said stonily.

'Ah, but it is,' he said with a tiny ironic quirk to his lips. 'When I saw you this afternoon I thought—that's incredible! The transformation from the plain, ultra-serious, intense ... *kid* that you were, to how you are now ... well, I thought, to be quite honest, that you must have found some man who'd made you very happy, chased away all the trauma. I suspected it was not so, unfortunately, a rather short time later.'

'Do you *really* think that's the answer?' she asked with a catch in her voice. 'You make it sound so simple. Throw yourself into some man's arms, Glamorgan, and all will be well! What a fairy tale,' she said contemptuously, 'My friend, I hate to have to tell you this, but I got over that near-rape surprisingly quickly. I mean, I can go to the cinema and watch Al Pacino or Dustin Hoffman making love to their respective ladies without throwing up—in fact I can even come away and think, now isn't that nice! What I can't do is find any man who doesn't have an ego the size of a football field and such a precarious sense of virility that it needs constant bolstering up and flattering until you feel, My God, why is it so fragile? What weapons do I have that I'm unaware of? What is it about a relatively defenceless female that seems to make men so vulnerable?'

He said after a moment, 'What a waste, Morgan. It really is a criminal waste to see you behind a desk selling package tours. You have a very fine brain, and that I never denied. But as to your passionate enquiry—could it be that you've never got to know a real man?'

She laughed in her throat. 'Are you proposing yourself? That's a joke, now, isn't it? And what is a real man, may I ask? My father was real enough. He was certainly strong enough to bully my mother into her grave, and believe me, I *know*, she was as true and faithful to him as the day was long. She married him and was stupid enough to think it was some kind of eternal bondage from which she could never escape. And he played on that mercilessly. Now that's a real man for you.'

'No,' he said gently, 'that was a deeply insecure man. A man not aware enough to rise above his insecurities. A man who should have been out fighting wars or chopping down trees instead of channelling all his insecurities and nervous energy into a lifetime of preaching and venting his frustration on you and your mother. Correct me if I'm wrong, but I got the impression that one of his dearest unfulfilled wishes was that he had a son.'

'How right you are,' she said bitterly. 'He even had his father's name, which also happened to be the name of his birthplace, picked out, and when I arrived he wouldn't hear of changing it! How else do you think I got stuck with this crazy name?'

'Is it crazy?' Steve asked gently. 'I rather like it. It makes me think of misty Welsh hillsides and valleys, clear cold streams and beautiful voices. I think it suits you. How is your father? Is he still alive?'

'So far as I know. At least he was last month. He went back to Wales to live with his brother a few years back. He still writes to me once a month and lately he's even intimated that he can see his way clear to forgive me for the shame and dishonour I heaped on his head.'

She closed her eyes tightly as she unwittingly relived that horrible, disastrous scene five years ago.

Her father had always been possessed of a quick, quite irrational temper and at first he had turned on Steven Harrow, assuming that he had assaulted her.

'Now why would I be bringing her home to you like this if I'd done it?' She remembered those words so clearly. Just as she remembered her father's sudden frightening silence for those few seconds before he had turned on her. And her stunned incredulity when he had attacked her harshly with his tongue and told her she'd deserved everything she'd got.

'Why . . . why do you say that?' she had stammered.

'Because women don't get raped for nothing,' he'd told her fiercely. 'Instead of concentrating on your studies you've been flaunting yourself, that's what!'

'But I haven't,' she had insisted in a trembling voice. 'I never have. All I did was agree to go to a party. The only mistake I made was to accept a lift home, and not from complete strangers either, but two people I knew . . . what was so wrong in that?'

'Wrong?' he had snorted fiercely. 'One young lass with two men who'd had a bit to drink—you don't see anything wrong in that?'

'Oh, Dad,' she'd said wearily. 'If you must know I
didn't realise they were that drunk until we were in the
car, and then I was far more worried about them driving
up a tree! They'd never given me a second glance in the
two years I'd known them. Nor has anyone else, for that
matter,' she had added, and flashed a suddenly furious
look at Steven Harrow who had been standing back
throughout the exchange with a peculiar look on his face.
'Why should anyone? I'm nothing much to look at and I
get around like second-hand Rose, thanks to your generosity. I know—I know you've reared me and all that and
are putting me through university, but I don't have to
be such a frump! If you didn't have such old-fashioned
ideas. . . .'

She had dropped her head into her hands then and
started to sob suddenly, completely overwhelmed.

It had been her father's contemptuous statement that
had brought her to her feet spitting with rage.

He had said coldly, 'Tears won't help you, Glamorgan.
This very night you've lost, thrown away, something so
precious, so. . . .'

'I have not lost my virginity!' she had shouted at him.
'Not that you'd care, but I fought tooth and nail, and all
it did was urge them on. But I still fought. Why do you
think I'm such a mess? Oh, I *hate* you!' she had sobbed as
she'd turned to limp painfully upstairs. 'And as for you,'
she'd added as her eyes fell on Steven Harrow and the
humiliation of this nasty little scene he had been forced to
witness on top of the rest had flooded her, 'as for you, the
very sight of you makes me sick!'

She came back to the present with a long shuddering
sigh and stared into the golden lamplight. A movement
beside her drew her fully back from the past and she was
surprised to see that he had made a pot of coffee while she
had been musing so painfully. He set the tray on the
wicker table and poured her a cup.

'And you never went back,' he said as he sat down with his own cup.

'No. Or didn't you notice?'

'I noted that a week later you hadn't returned. That was about the start of the summer vacation, if you recall, and up until then I'd been knee deep in examination papers. No one could have been more astonished, when I checked with the Dean of the Faculty, than I was to discover that your father hadn't even made a complaint. So I went to see you, but you'd gone—on holiday, according to the neighbours. That's when I started to make a few enquiries among your fellow students. But there wasn't much I could do without you to identify the two. And it was at the end of that term that I took off for Oxford.'

'Oh,' was all she could find to say. Then, stiffly, 'Well, it was kind of you to take the trouble. But although I didn't agree with my father's thoughts on the subject, my final decision was the same as his, I knew I couldn't go back and face you all. So I got a job in an office and took a course in travel and another one at a charm school where they taught me how to dress and walk and care for my skin. And twelve months later I got my present job.'

'Do you write to your father?' he asked.

She hesitated for a moment, then she said ungraciously, 'Yes. Also once a month. But only because I know my mother would have wanted me to. And anyway, I did manage to break away from him. And . . . and someone once told me that you can only call yourself really mature when you don't blame all your problems on your father or your teacher or your Prime Minister . . .' She broke off and smiled suddenly, with a tiny wry twist of her lips. 'It sounds funny, doesn't it?'

He smiled back. 'Yes, it does. It's probably true though. Are you working on it?'

She nodded, but added sardonically, 'I was doing well too, until you came back into my life.'

'I wonder,' he said dryly. 'Tell you what, when you can feel relaxed and easy in my company then you'll know you've passed the test.'

Morgan thought about that for a long moment with her hazel eyes down and her long lashes casting shadows on her cheeks. At last she said huskily, 'I don't see the point. I'm sure you don't mix with women on a purely platonic basis unless you happen to be working with them or . . . unless they happen to be married to or spoken for by a friend of yours. Otherwise it seems like a pointless exercise.'

Steve chewed his lip, his eyes never leaving hers. Finally he raised his eyebrows and said lightly, 'What do you do at the weekends?'

'Plenty,' she said shortly.

'I'll tell you why,' he went on imperturbably. 'I'm writing a novel—at the weekends, that is. I find it helps me from getting stale on my thesis.' He raised one clenched fist to his mouth and chewed his knuckle thoughtfully, an action that took Morgan back so vividly to her student memories of him that she breathed deeply. 'But I need a research assistant,' he went on. 'And someone to kind of restore a bit of order to what I've written so far. I mean, it's all scattered around loose, un-corrected, and to put it mildly, in a hell of a mess. I'd pay you by the hour, and also travelling expenses.'

'Do you mean the whole weekend?' she asked incredu-lously.

'No, either Saturdays or Sundays, whichever suited you. Do you mean you'll do it?'

'I . . . no! I mean, I'd have to think about it,' she said disjointedly.

'Well, that's a start.' Steve grinned and reached for the crystal decanter. 'Another brandy? You still look a bit pale.'

'No, thank you. I have to drive home, remember?'

'No, you don't,' he said easily. 'In fact I wouldn't dream of allowing you to after . . . all this.'

'You . . . *you* wouldn't allow it!' She sat upright and stared at him outraged. 'You can't do anything to stop me, Steven Harrow!'

'I wouldn't be too sure of that,' he drawled. 'And call me Steve,' he added with a slow smile. 'All my friends do. But I have no intention of allowing you to negotiate that road down the hill at this time of night. And that's not a reflection on your driving, Morgan, merely a reflection on the road, *if* you can call it that.'

She opened and closed her mouth rather like a fish out of water, but no words would come.

He regarded her amusedly for some time before he burst out laughing. 'What are you trying to say?' he asked. 'I can assure you no one will think you compromised in any way because no one will know you're here, should they have nasty little minds like that anyway. And what's more, I intend to spend the night on the couch,' he gestured to the magnificent leather settee. 'I often do, as a matter of fact, when I fall asleep watching television. It's very comfortable, and you can have the bed all to yourself.' He shrugged. 'You're welcome to lock yourself in if that's what you're worried about,' he added casually.

'But . . . but . . .' Morgan spluttered, and took a deep breath to regain her composure. 'Look,' she said coolly at last, 'I appreciate your concern. It's not possible, though. I have no clothes but the ones I'm wearing, and I'm not in the habit of going to work in yesterday's clothes.'

'Ah,' he said, and tapped his teeth with a forefinger. 'Now that is a slight problem, I admit. But not insoluble. Do you wear that same uniform every day? Rather, an identical one,' he amended amiably with a gesture that made her long to be able to hit him. 'I know, you've already told me you don't wear yesterday's clothes. But do you?'

'Yes, I do,' she said through her teeth. 'Are you able to conjure one up?' she enquired sweetly. 'Or are you going to suggest that I hare home tomorrow morning at the crack of dawn, to the other side of town, I might just add, and throw on my clothes and then hare off to work? Because it's not on,' she said flatly.

'Neither of those. But you see I'm incredibly domesticated here in my little mountain eyrie, Morgan. I'm possessed of not only a twin-tub washing machine but also a tumble dryer. You could wash out your undies and your blouse and pop them into the dryer and the whole operation would be accomplished in no time at all. Do you wash your skirt and jacket out after each wearing?'

'No,' she said involuntarily, 'I usually press them and . . .' She stopped short and closed her eyes and pinched herself figuratively. I must be mad, she thought wearily, quite mad to even engage in this discussion with him. But then again I always knew—somehow—that he wasn't the kind of man who cut himself off from purely feminine matters . . . like my father. I always knew that. I just can't work out how I knew it! How I know, for example, that if anyone were ever to have his baby, he'd be deeply interested in every aspect of that pregnancy and be there to hold your hand at the birth.

She sprang up agitatedly. I am mad, she told herself angrily.

'Look,' she said fiercely, 'I'm not. . . .'

'Yes, you are, Morgan,' he interrupted smoothly, and stood up too.

She backed away as he towered over her. He didn't follow her, but his sheer size made her moisten her lips anxiously. She came to an abrupt decision. 'All right,' she said tautly, and finding herself with her chair right behind her knees, she sat down rather thankfully. 'Don't imagine,' she continued acidly, 'that I'm going to indulge in a little test of strength with you. I'd rather die than give you that kind of satisfaction, my *friend*. But I can tell you this—I'll certainly think twice before I ever set foot inside here again. So it might be an idea to advertise for your precious research secretary!'

'Well now,' he said smoothly, 'you made the right decision. You wouldn't have enjoyed the drive home, not feeling as upset as you do. And I'd have hated to have you on my conscience for a second time. Look, do you think you're mature enough to accept it now and put aside all your prickliness? I assure you I have no designs on you,' he said pointedly, 'so why can't we enjoy the rest of the evening? We used to be able to commune very well on a purely intellectual level . . . once. Why shouldn't we try it again?'

Morgan swallowed uneasily and stared at her beautifully manicured hands that were so different from how they used to be. 'Very well,' she said quietly. 'Since I have no choice, so be it.'

She looked up, fully expecting to see his eyes full of laughter, but they were expressionless and even hooded. He turned away.

'That's my girl,' he said tonelessly.

CHAPTER THREE

So be it. Her own words seemed to echo in her head throughout the rest of the evening. I can't help but feel like Alice in Wonderland, she thought as Steve helped her to operate the washing machine a little later after she had had a warm bath in his sumptuous bathroom and donned one of his T-shirts and a burgundy-coloured towelling robe with short sleeves that reached halfway down her arms.

I mean in the context, she reminded herself militantly, that it's all like a dream. A most unusual dream too. If anyone had told me this morning what was in store for me tonight I'd have. . . .

Laughed? she asked herself, and winced. For at that moment she could vividly picture Ryan's laughing face. If he but knew, she thought dismally. What was it I said? Something foolish about being in total command? Oh, Morgan!

And yet she had to admit that the rest of the evening wasn't a total penance for her. They had attended to her washing and then done the dishes in Steve's ultra-modern kitchen. Mundane enough chores, but an unexpected treat had come when he had taken her into his study and shown her his thesis.

She had been quite unprepared for the very real wash of interest and genuine delight that she had been unable to stifle at this glimpse of pure academic science.

'I . . . I always had a hankering after Anthropology,' she admitted finally after being unable to show herself as anything but completely absorbed as he spoke.

He cast her a look of sudden surprise. 'Well, why didn't

you take it?' he asked.

'My father,' she said with a swift upward glance. 'He didn't think it was quite ladylike you know, to be exploring uncivilised people's sexual habits and so on. He didn't understand. . . .'

'Don't tell me,' he warned with a sudden grin. 'I suppose he imagined you'd want to go out and practise with the natives. Not really? *Really?*' He laughed then. 'Dear God, it's amazing how tenaciously some people cling to their so cherished preconceived ideas!'

'Do you—I mean, do you think it's a lack of education that makes people so rigid, so. . . .' Morgan sought for the right words, but couldn't find them.

'So *so?*' he supplied. 'Not altogether. I've known humble shepherds who've never been inside a schoolroom but who've had a basic philosophy of peace and how to co-exist with your fellow men and your environment that far transcends anything I could ever aspire to. How do they get it? I'm not sure. I think it probably has something to do with genes, family background and one's expectations. And there,' he said sombrely, 'we're at a slight disadvantage.'

'You mean people like us, like my father, couldn't keep pace with his expectations. I mean that he had too broad a scope. That, for example, the shepherd would not have had?'

'Something like that. But then again I'm sure there are simple shepherds who are less than competent. It's . . . I guess it's one of the big questions, Morgan. Perhaps every age since the beginning of time has been plagued and worried about the number of misfits and malcontents it produces.'

'Perhaps,' she said with a smile. 'What right do we have to imagine we're exclusive? Do you know, the happiest person I ever met was a bee-keeper, of all things. Not full-time, in fact his full-time job was unbelievably dull. He was a storeman in a nut and bolt factory. But this thing he had about bees was incredible. And he enjoyed every minute of his life, even when he was away from his precious swarm, because then he could look forward to seeing them again. He even wrote a little book and financed its publication out of his overtime.'

'Now, there you've put your finger on it,' Steve said seriously. 'Those kind of people are the luckiest of all.'

'Are you . . . aren't you . . . one of them?' Morgan asked tentatively.

He shrugged. 'Not entirely,' he said sombrely. 'Believe me, I too tried to take on the world single-handed, tried to fight it and change some of its rigid, narrow principles, but I didn't succeed notably.'

'Oh? How?'

He considered for a moment. 'I don't think I'll tell you that, Miss Bright Eyes,' he said lightly. 'That's part of another instalment.'

'Oh, really?' she said caustically. 'Well then, I shall have to miss it, shan't I?'

'Not have to. It's quite up to you.' He glanced at his watch. 'Hell! Do you know what the time is? Midnight. And I think time for our working girl to get her beauty sleep.'

'Very well,' she replied equably. 'Goodnight, Steve.'

'Goodnight, Morgan,' he said gravely. 'Sweet dreams.'

But surprisingly she didn't dream at all, although it was some time before she fell asleep. The big bed was superbly comfortable once she had remade it and she lay there for a while, unwilling to turn the lamp off.

She tried to analyse this unwillingness. Was it due to the strange mixture of sounds floating into the bedroom that were so unlike the night sounds she was accustomed to? The rustling of leaves, the throb of a cricket and the unmistakable sounds of Steve Harrow moving round quietly.

She thought of her little flat in the suburb of Herston which was not far from the Children's Hospital. The flat was small but modern in a block of six that stood out rather incongruously in a sea of old, distinctive Queensland homes. It wasn't a particularly quiet area or a fashionable one, but it had the advantage of being close to the city centre and in the two years she had been there she had made quite a few acquaintances in the street and felt herself at home.

And while her flat's decor didn't aspire to these heights, she thought as she moved luxuriously on the finest percale sheets and glanced around the room to note the unexpected touches she'd missed earlier, she wasn't dissatisfied with it either. Her flat was pleasant and homely, and if most of the furniture was second-hand, it had been interesting and lovingly restored. In fact she was quite an expert with sandpaper and enamel and the odd screw and nail.

But I would adore to have that at home, she thought drowsily as she stared at the magnificent oil painting on the wall opposite the bed. It was a landscape that brought to life the character of the Australian bush in all its subtle tonings. There were no emerald greens or vivid blues in this painting, but the duller greens and sandy tones and the lion-coloured grass and the grey and stark white gum tree trunks that were so real she felt almost as if she could smell the outback as she'd seen and smelt it on one never-to-be-forgotten trip to the Boulia triangle of Western Queensland.

I shall dream of the Min Min lights, she thought sleepily, thinking of that unexpected phenomenon that had put the fear of God into so many travellers caught at night in that vast, sparsely populated area around

Longreach, Winton and Boulia. If I turn the lamp off and throw that landscape into darkness, before long those powerful, mysterious lights will come from nowhere.

She shivered slightly and didn't turn the lamp off but stroked the cabinet beside the bed instead. For it contained another refinement she would very much like to own—a magnificent stereo record and tape deck.

He had shown it to her earlier and pointed out the speakers cunningly built into the ceiling. He had also shown her how to use it and given her a demonstration with a tape of a piece of music she had never heard before. A piece she could only describe as the most evocative music she had ever heard, evocative of jungle and strange, brilliantly plumed birds and native drums and a broad silent river that had seemed to fill the room from every corner.

Now, Morgan, she told herself firmly, you're being fanciful, kid. Instead of worrying about the Min Min lights and the lurking dangers of the Amazon Basin you should really be thinking about your host. And just how you managed to miscalculate so completely and to the extent that you're here now, lying in his bed wearing his pyjama top. . . .

She drew her knees up and fingered the violet-coloured sheet delicately. Then she turned on her side and pushed one arm beneath the soft, plump pillows, revelling in the feel of cool cotton on her skin.

And finally she fell asleep with her limbs sprawled sensuously, because somehow this bed made her feel that way, and with her chestnut hair spread across the pillows, and the lamp still on.

She woke just as the dawn started to lighten the rim of the eastern horizon. It was a kookaburra that woke her. He began to laugh and broke off midway as if conscious that it was a bit early for his strident call. But two

minutes later he started again, and this time one of his
mates joined in and Morgan sat and laughed to herself
with pleasure.

Then she scrambled out of bed, and pulled on
the towelling robe and slipped out on to the wooden
deck.

And jumped as a voice said out of the near-darkness,
'Morning, Glamorgan. Pull up a chair and join me for
the concert and the sunrise.'

She did, and was enchanted as the darkness dissolved
and the whole Moreton region rolled away to the sea from
the base of Mount Nebo beneath her feet to the accompaniment of kookaburras and warbling magpies, annoyed-
sounding plovers and several other varieties she could not
identify. And one lone rooster sounding uncertain and
reedy.

She burst out laughing. 'He sounds so out of place . . .
that rooster, I mean. Do you think he's escaped from
someone's backyard and taken a trip up here?'

'As a matter of fact he has. But not of his own accord.
That's Sylvester, a chum of mine, and don't you dare tell
him he sounds out of place. He has enough complexes as
it is.'

She eyed him. 'Do you keep chickens?'

'Uh-huh. I've levelled out a bit of ground at the back
of the house and am trying—rather unsuccessfully—to
grow vegetables and rear chickens. I acquired Sylvester
because I thought he might stimulate my hens to lay a
little more prolifically. However, he seems to have the
opposite effect. Far from welcoming him they tried to
peck him to death. He's still attempting to regain his male
ego.'

'Are you serious?' she demanded. 'It sounds like a tall
tale to me.'

'Well, perhaps a bit of an overstatement,' Steve
conceded. 'These glorious mornings seem to have that

effect on me.' He breathed deeply of the champagne-clear air.

'It's very beautiful,' she said idly, and let her gaze sweep the panorama below her. 'I can't imagine how you get any work done up here. It would distract me, I'm sure.'

'You get used to it—in part. Not the sunrise, though.' Steve stood up and stretched so that the lean taut lines of his torso were clearly visible beneath his clinging cotton-knit shirt and well-fitting jeans.

Morgan closed her eyes involuntarily and opened them to concentrate her gaze on his bare feet. 'Shall I make breakfast?' she asked politely. 'I mean, do you eat breakfast? I do,' she hurried on. 'I adore breakfast. I'd rather miss out on any other meal of the day.' Stop gabbling, Morgan! she commanded herself nervously. He might remind you of Apollo—or is it Adonis?—but I bet if you pricked him he'd be like every other man beneath the surface.

She raised her eyes to find him looking at her quizzically.

'Why are you looking at me like that?' she asked crossly.

'. . . . Because I'm delighted,' he said after a moment. 'That's another thing we have in common—Anthropology and a liking for a good hearty breakfast.' He held his arm down to her. 'Lead on, Lady Macduff. You may culinate in luxury! We have a choice of bacon and eggs or sausages and eggs—or all three if you so desire.'

'Is there such a word as culinate?' she asked with a giggle she couldn't repress.

'Who knows? If there wasn't, there is now. I shall make immediate representation to that august body, whoever they are—I mean the one that compiles the Oxford English Dictionary—to have it included forthwith. At least among the section that deals so patronisingly with Australianisms!'

She was still laughing softly to herself as she moved about the kitchen. If you thought you were mad before, Morgan, you've got to admit you've progressed one step farther now. What would you call the next step? Insanity? Lunacy?

'I don't honestly know,' she mused out aloud. 'Perhaps I'm just drunk on sunrise and birdsong.' She turned the sizzling sausages in the pan and then wandered into the lounge to set the table.

Steve was not in evidence, but she could hear the shower gushing. She looked around the room and then blushed vividly. For displayed upon one aquamarine chair with the skill of an expert window dresser were her lacy bra and panties and her pale tights cunningly draped in a waterfall of folds.

She reached out and snatched them up. She had forgotten about them and her blouse whirling around in the tumble dryer when she'd gone to bed. But it seemed Steve had not. Her blouse was hanging on a hanger from a doorknob close by and her skirt and jacket from another doorknob.

Well, he was taking things a little too much for granted, she thought rebelliously as she bundled them all into the bedroom and then retreated hastily as she heard the shower being switched off.

She stood in the middle of the lounge, her brow furrowed in a painful frown. Oh, Morgan! She breathed deeply. Oh, Morgan, what a fool you are! You're poised once more at the lip of the same precipice. How did you let it happen?

'I didn't,' she said softly to herself. 'It must be a bit like malaria—a recurring fever. Yes, that's what it is. But no, that's a stupid analogy. I have so many weapons in my armoury now. I have a stimulating, enjoyable job, despite his thinking it a waste. I have some money in the bank and I can afford to take an interesting vacation once a year, run a car and wear expensive clothes. What more could I want?

What more? she answered herself wordlessly. Certainly not the silly kind of agony I went through last time. And even then I didn't have the added spur in my flesh of 'being on his conscience'!

Oh no! I proved it once that out of sight is out of mind. I can do it again.

She sniffed suddenly and then fled into the kitchen to deal with the sausages.

'How long,' she asked conversationally as she munched her toast, 'do you think it will take me to get into town?'

'At this time of day, a good hour, I reckon.' Steve pushed his plate away and glinted a smile across at her. 'Very enjoyable,' he commented. 'You're not a bad cook yourself.'

'Do you think sausages and eggs are a real test?'

'Perhaps not. Why don't you invite me to dinner one night and . . . consolidate your position?'

'I'll think about it,' she answered lightly, and sprang up. 'If you don't mind, I also think I'll get ready and, as they say, hit the track! I threatened Ryan with murder if he was late this morning, so I ought not set a bad example myself.'

'Ryan?' he said lazily, still sprawled back in his chair. 'Is that your colleague? The bright, inquisitive Mr Clarke?'

'The same,' she said ruefully.

'Is he married?' he queried.

'No. Why do you ask?'

'Just out of curiosity, I guess. Do you think he'd like to be married to you?' he asked, his blue eyes suddenly uncomfortably probing.

'Ryan,' she said tartly, 'would probably run a mile if anyone tried to put a noose and halter on him. I don't think he's progressed beyond the heavy dalliance stage yet.'

He grinned up at her. 'Has he ever tried to dally with you?'

'Frequently,' she said flatly. 'At least once a day. But for all that,' she relented slightly, 'he's not a bad kid.'

She turned on her heel and marched into the bedroom, ignoring his wryly muttered comment, 'Poor Ryan!'

It was while she was in the sumptuous bathroom, fully dressed but attending to the last details of her grooming, that Steve shouldered the door open and stood watching her. Their eyes met once in the mirror, then she moved slightly and concentrated deliberately on doing the best she could with the limited resources her small cosmetic purse contained.

It wasn't that she wore a lot of make-up, but what little she did wear she liked to be able to apply expertly, and the contents of her cosmetic purse which she carried around in her handbag were only sufficient really to effect running repairs.

Still, she reflected, she had a tiny tube of moisturizer, some mascara and the bright, deep lipstick that was all the rage currently. And a small, purse-size brush.

But she found that her hands weren't quite steady as she tried to stroke her eyebrows, that were beautifully shaped naturally, into perfect order. If only he'd go away, she thought, but if I ask him to, he'll realise he's making me nervous, and I don't intend to give him that satisfaction.

She brushed her hair vigorously, then smoothed it down with her fingers and straightened her collar beneath its sweeping fall.

'There,' she said, and turned away from the mirror.

'What about this?' asked Steve, and held out the tube of lipstick.

She all but snatched it out of his hand and said hastily, 'I'll put it on when I get to work.'

'Oh,' he said as she turned away from him, then she felt his hands on her shoulders turning her back to meet his blue, blue gaze.

'Mmm,' he said approvingly. 'You look beautiful and very, very expensive, Morgan. Like some hothouse bloom.' He went on as she coloured faintly, his eyes tracking the delicate rose colour that came to her cheeks with a curiously intent look, 'Have you thought about my proposition? Whether you'd like to work for me?'

Say no, Morgan. No, no, no! Just say it straight out, she commanded herself. But with her pulses suddenly leaping at his proximity and her heart thudding painfully at the feel of his hands on her shoulders like a searing brand through the thin stuff of her blouse, she found she couldn't say anything for a long moment—found that all she wanted to do was reach out and touch the strong lines of his throat. And worse—that she'd like to unbutton her blouse and guide his lean strong fingers to the valley between her breasts.

'I . . . I'll . . . I'd like to think about it some more,' she stammered. 'Are you on the phone?' she asked, desperately trying to regain some sort of composure.

He dropped his hands and shoved them into the pockets of his jeans. 'Yeah,' he said casually, 'that's an idea. Give me a ring some time. There's no real urgency.'

Morgan could never afterwards understand what made her try to lend an air of authenticity to her little deception. Because she had no intention of ever seeing Steve again or even talking to him on the phone. But she said, 'You're not taking off for some distant pasture in the next few days? I mean, you will be home?'

'Oh yes,' he said with ironically raised eyebrows that made her feel uncomfortably that he'd seen right through her little ploy. 'I'll be here.'

'Good,' she forced herself to say briskly. She reached for her purse. 'Now I really ought to get going. 'Thank you,' she added over her shoulder as she walked as steadily as she could through to the lounge. 'I can't say I enjoyed it all, but the view and the sunrise and the meal were superb.'

He shrugged. 'Any time, Glamorgan. Any time.'

He knows, she thought, as she steered the little car down the rough track from the house. He knows I won't be back. She took one clammy hand from the steering wheel and wiped it on the towelling seat cover beside her. And I think he's going to accept it, she mused as her mind flicked back to the low-key farewells they had just exchanged. She had turned once as she drove away, to see that he hadn't even waited until she was out of sight before he had gone back inside.

So that's that, she congratulated herself. You did it, Morgan.

And this curious flavour of desolation you're tasting will surely pass. But a measure of its potency only dawned on her a little later when she realised she had driven down Mount Nebo and through the Gap unseeing of the views and aware only of the road beneath her wheels.

Ryan was there before her, working busily at his desk. She glanced at her watch to see that it was only eight-fifteen. They didn't open until eight-thirty.

'You're early,' she said as she took off her jacket and hung it up.

'Mmm. There!' He looked up. 'I've finished my home-work.' He held out a sheet of paper to her. 'Old Mr Wallace's fare quotation. Hey!' He looked at her with his head on one side.

'What is it?' she asked absently as she studied the sheet.

'You forgot your lipstick, Morgan. Don't tell me you had such a late night with your ex-lecturer that you found it a little difficult to get yourself together this morning?' he said, his eyes bright with interest.

She blinked and touched a finger to her lips. Of course! She'd forgotten all about it. But she said coolly, 'So I have. Never mind, I'll put it on after I've had a cup of coffee. Would you like one?'

'Thank you,' he said gravely. 'I gather the subject is closed.'

She turned her hazel eyes to him and thought thankfully that at least here was one male she could handle. 'What subject?' she asked flatly. 'By the way, this isn't a bad quotation. I can think of only one improvement.'

'I see,' he said, and nodded. 'Very well,' he added with a slight quirk tugging at his lips, 'I shall say no more.'

And he was as good as his word for once, although Morgan was aware that he looked at her quizzically every now and then through the rest of that long day.

A week went past surprisingly slowly and then another, during which she managed to feel more relaxed as she tore each day from her desk calendar and was even able occasionally to wonder whether she had dreamed the whole business.

But on the last two days of the fortnight she received two shocks that set her precarious calm back considerably.

The first came in the form of a letter from her uncle in Wales, informing her that her father was suffering from an unusual complaint that required an intricate operation and a long convalescence to cure it.

She had never met her uncle, but his phrases somehow called vividly to mind her father's Welsh accent which he had never entirely lost in all his years in Australia.

She re-read the rolling phrases a little dazedly. It appeared he could have the operation on the National Health but was stubbornly refusing to be herded around 'like some sick head of cattle'. The heavy quotation marks are unnecessary, Morgan thought. I can just hear him saying it.

'. . . . This is not an entirely accurate description,' her unseen uncle wrote. 'In fact in all honesty I must admit it's possibly highly inaccurate and I'm sure he would receive the best of treatment without having to lay out a penny, although he wouldn't be able to maintain his cherished privacy. But he's a stubborn man, as you may know, and has decided that he will either lick his wounds in his lair or not at all—certainly not beneath the scrutiny of a public ward. I've had word with his doctors and they deem the operation essential if he's not to have a curtailed lifespan spent in increasing discomfort which is already becoming evident. And so I thought to write to you, dearest niece, for your advice, as the only other close relative he has in the world. . . .'

Morgan bit her lip and after work that day went to visit her mother's grave. As she stood there in the growing chilly dusk, she recalled her mother's often said words: There's one thing you can't change . . . ever, Glamorgan. He's your father. There's him in you and you in him.

She closed her eyes. I've got my whole life ahead of me, she thought. And maybe, just maybe he was the way he was because he cared too much. I doubt it I'll ever know, though, she thought wryly a moment later. I don't suppose he could ever tell me. That was the core of the problem . . . perhaps. She sighed deeply once and pulled her jacket more closely around her.

The next morning she went to her bank and arranged for a bank draft to be transmitted overseas for an amount that virtually cleaned her account out. But although she knew she couldn't have rested in peace if she hadn't done it, as she stared at the new balance in her book, she felt a shiver of insecurity.

Well, it won't take me five years to build up that total again, she reassured herself. But nonetheless, I feel somehow naked without it.

The second surprise that awaited her was something she literally tripped over as she fumbled in her purse for the key to her flat that same evening. Steven Harrow was squatting patiently on the concrete walkway beside her front door.

Morgan turned alternately red and white and demanded furiously, 'What on earth are you doing here?'

'Come to see you,' he said blandly as he rose and dusted himself off. 'I've been expecting a phone call from you,' he added reproachfully.

She ground her teeth. 'Oh, rubbish! You knew very well I wasn't going to ring you. I mean, where are we—in some kindergarten?'

He raised his eyebrows laughingly. 'Perhaps.'

'Well, all right, I'll spell it out for you. I don't want your job. I don't want to be on your conscience. And don't tell me,' she added menacingly, 'that you went through all the Joneses in the telephone book!'

'No,' he admitted. 'I went through Ryan Clarke—a most willing accomplice I found.' He wrested the key from her grasp and calmly unlocked the door. 'After you, ma'am,' he murmured graciously.

Morgan cast him a blazing look from beneath her lashes, but after a slight hesitation she stalked into the flat. He followed her into the lounge and stood in the middle of the room, dwarfing it somewhat just as he'd dwarfed her car.

He looked around and observed conversationally, 'Nice place you have here.'

'I hate you!' she said through her teeth. 'You have no right to come here and hound me to death!' She flung her purse on the small cane settee with its bright floral cushions and they bent simultaneously to retrieve the three envelopes she had collected from her mailbox and forgotten she was clutching too.

She moved away as if scalded as their hands touched, but the quick movement unbalanced her and she ended up sitting in an undignified heap on the floor with Steve kneeling beside her.

'Are you hurt, Morgan?' he asked softly, his blue eyes with their depths of hidden laughter only inches from her own furious hazel ones. 'Here, let me help you up,' he added smoothly, and gravely assisted her to a chair despite her efforts to fend him off.

She took a deep breath and clenched her fists as he knelt down again and ran his hands over her legs from below the knee to her ankles. 'Model girl legs,' he said admiringly, 'but you should take greater care on these delicate heels. You might have sprained your ankle.' He removed one of her elegant high-heeled shoes and twisted her foot gently from side to side.

'Will you take your hands off me,' she said coldly. 'What makes you think you have some inalienable right to undress me whenever you feel like it?' she demanded.

'I wouldn't call this undressing you, precisely,' he drawled as he slipped the shoe on again. 'More like being a good Samaritan.' He stood up and dropped the envelopes into her lap. 'Your mail,' he said politely. 'Doesn't look too promising, I'm afraid. Those window envelopes rarely do, have you noticed?'

'I. . . .' Morgan started to say something cutting, but her eyes narrowed as the full import of her words sank in and she glanced down at the mail in her lap. She bit her lip and repressed a groan. She didn't need to open them to know what they were—her telephone account and annual rental, her car registration renewal, and the third one peeping coyly out from behind the other two looked suspiciously like the bill for the recent overhaul she'd had done on the car.

That does it, she thought miserably. That cleans me out of just about every penny I have left. I just hope to God the electricity bill isn't due this month!

'What is it, Morgan?'

She jumped and looked up to see Steve Harrow staring down at her curiously. She'd forgotten for a moment that he was there.

'I . . . it's nothing,' she said tonelessly as she made an effort to collect her scattered wits. 'I usually have a cup of tea at this time of day. Would you like one—before you hit the road?' she added pointedly, and stood up.

He grinned. 'Never say no to a cuppa! What's in there, though,' he nodded towards the envelopes now reposing on the small gateleg table that served as her dining table, 'that brought about the change of front? Bad news?'

'Not really,' she managed to say casually. 'Nothing I can't handle.' She moved into her tiny kitchen and filled the kettle. Steve followed her and stood leaning against the doorjamb with his arms folded across his chest.

'A slight setback?' he queried. 'Perhaps of a financial nature?' he hazarded.

Morgan couldn't prevent the sudden glance she shot him. He's too damned acute, she thought resentfully. But she managed to say lightly, 'Perhaps. But only of a very temporary nature.' She assembled the tea tray and poured the now boiling water into the teapot. She lifted the tray and Steve stood aside.

She said over her shoulder as she moved into the lounge, 'I might be wasting my brains, but at least I have the advantage of being well paid for it.'

'I didn't imagine you were destitute,' he said coolly with one eyebrow raised. 'Unless you have some un-suspected vices. Are you a mad gambler?'

She pulled out two chairs and sat down herself. 'Have a seat,' she said casually. 'No, I'm not. Mind you, I do enjoy an afternoon at the races, but not to punt.'

'What for, then?' he asked quizzically, as he helped himself to two of the oatmeal cookies from the biscuit barrel.

'Yes, do have . . . some,' she said sweetly. 'I like watching the horses, as a matter of fact. In *fact* I was thinking of buying a share. . . .' She stopped abruptly and then had to smile ruefully to herself. That little dream would have to wait too. Not that it would have been possible just yet anyway.

'Thinking of buying a share in a racehorse? It's big business, this syndication deal, these days, but you'd want to have your wits about you, Morgan.' His quizzical tones intruded on her reflections.

'I know that,' she said with a scathing look from her clear hazel eyes. 'I don't understand why men always think they have to talk down to women on just about every subject other than formulas and nappies!'

Steve contemplated her thoughtfully for a long moment, then he lowered his golden tipped lashes and said evenly, 'Ah. But I do understand why you're so particularly sensitive about it, you see. You. . . .'

She cut in abruptly, 'Now don't start on that subject again! It's closed! You may think you're omnipotent for all I care. I'm simply not interested in discussing it.'

'But you do admit that you're in a little financial jam? I mean, I did hear you say that?' he asked, suddenly relentless, as she shook her head impatiently. 'Did you or did you not say that, Morgan?' he demanded with a tinge of impatience. 'Or are you trying to tell me that because I'm a *man* my hearing must be defective?'

She raised her hand in a disclaiming gesture, but he caught her wrist and bore it inexorably down to the table. '*Answer* me, Morgan,' he said tautly as his eyes bored into her own.

'With great pleasure,' she said icily, emphasising each word, 'as soon as you let my wrist go.'

She rubbed her wrist resentfully as his fingers released it. 'It's like this,' she said slowly and evenly as if she were speaking to a five-year-old. 'I have plenty for my daily needs. I can well afford my rent, my clothes and my food and even my car. But owing to unforeseen circumstance I have nothing in reserve now. Which only means that I shall have to skip my holiday this year, possibly have to make do with last winter's wardrobe which I might have done in any case because I happen to like it, and not be able to indulge my passion for owning a share in a horse. And for your information, before this happened I was still several years away from *that* dream and hadn't entirely made up my mind as to which was the better investment, horseflesh or real estate.'

They gazed at each other wordlessly for a long moment until she said at last and as patronisingly as she could, 'Do you understand?'

'I do,' Steve said softly and almost to himself as he grimaced wryly. 'You have your future very firmly mapped out, don't you, Morgan? Like a man?'

'Wh—what do you mean?'

'I mean that you're making damned sure that you never have to depend on any man ever. Consciously or unconsciously you've opted for the single life, haven't you? The lonely road.'

Morgan tossed her head but lowered her eyes suddenly. 'It's none of your business if I have. *If* I have, and there you're assuming a great deal. Why shouldn't I bother about my future? It could do no harm even if I did get married.'

'None at all,' he said ironically. 'And what's more, your little nest egg would always be there, handy somewhere so that you could back out if ever the going got too rough.'

'Of course,' she said, equally ironic, 'that's not really done, is it? I mean, it's only men who are allowed to have those kind of boltholes.'

'That's what puzzles me,' he said after a moment. 'Here I am offering you an interesting opportunity of augmenting your income and at the same time an opportunity to score off me. There's only one reason that I can think of for your refusal.'

She sat back and eyed him. 'What's that?' she asked wearily.

'This,' he said quietly, and laid his hand on her forearm.

She tensed immediately and then forced herself to relax.

'You're afraid, Morgan. Afraid you can't trust yourself with me. Afraid that you haven't grown out of that adolescent crush—that maybe you never will.'

Her immediate response was involuntary, but even as she uttered it, she knew with a bitter self-knowledge that he had hit the nail on the head with unerring accuracy.

'Nonsense,' she said, not forcefully but quite as if the idea even surprised her a little. 'You know,' she went on with a barely perceptible pause, and put her head to one side assessingly, 'I . . . I'm a little disappointed. I must admit I thought you were a class above the . . . Ryans of this world. I did think you might have progressed beyond the stage of . . . of . . .' she sought for the right words, 'I don't know . . . of feeling that if every passable girl didn't drool at the mere thought of your masculinity, you'd failed somehow and had to erect a defence mechanism. You know, make out that she's one kind of a nut if not the other.'

Steve's sudden jolt of laughter cut her off effectively. 'Oh, Morgan,' he said, 'you're a delight to me. A confirmed cynic—but such a gorgeous one! I can't help but find it a little refreshing, I must say.'

'Oh, Steve,' she mimicked his tone, 'if you knew what an old line that was, mate! I reckon Ryan Clarke fell out of his cradle knowing that one.'

The silence that greeted her words stretched. She refused to drop her eyes, but then so did he, and it was he who finally broke it.

'Why don't you pick up the ... gauntlet, then, Glamorgan?' he asked softly but with a peculiar light in his blue eyes.

'Because I don't fancy being treated like a classic, clinical case of frigidity,' she answered equally softly, 'or, to put it into your terms, to be treated like a stunted landscape, blighted and unproductive until you work out how to alter the watershed. Oh no—there are easier ways of earning a dollar. And actually I have a few up my sleeve. I already tutor a few children in the street and babysit a few more.' She did not add that she had steadfastly refused payment for these duties that had been more in the nature of pleasure to her. She tilted her chin at him and shrugged. 'Maybe not as lucrative as your job, but very satisfying.'

He lifted his eyebrows lazily and tapped his teeth. 'I've got two nephews,' he offered. 'They're twelve and nine. I could borrow them occasionally to liven the place up.'

Morgan took a deep breath. 'I'm not. . . .' She started to speak steadily, but stopped and shrugged suddenly. 'Very well, I will,' she heard herself say with some inner amazement. 'I'll do it for six weeks providing you pay me five dollars an hour and pay for my petrol.' She stared at him expressionlessly.

'Spoken like a true blue,' he shrugged. 'You're on, then, Morgan. How about this Saturday, say from ten to four?'

'O.K.' She eyed him as he stood up. 'I hope you're not planning to hitch a ride home with me tonight?'

He grinned and his eyes sparkled blue fire. 'I wouldn't dare! I have too much respect for my person. See you

Saturday, kid.' And with a negligent wave he left the flat.

Morgan took her cup to the lounge window.

'I'm mad,' she told herself as she watched his tall lithe figure below her striding along the pavement. 'But then again,' she sighed heavily, 'isn't that how inoculation works? A small dose of the virus activates all the antibodies? Perhaps it's just what I need!' She turned away impatiently as Steve Harrow disappeared round a corner.

CHAPTER FOUR

MORGAN took no notice of Ryan's wary glances the next morning. In fact she worked hard at being perfectly normal, and it was only after lunch that she realised she had worked too hard at it.

He said to her pleadingly apropos of nothing, 'Does this mean you're going to forgive me, Morgan?'

She raised her eyebrows, but caught the look of enquiring innocence on her face before it took hold, and buried it. After all, she thought, one can get into a habit of concealing the truth from other people very easily. And the next step—concealing it from yourself—kind of follows. And that, above all things, is what I want to avoid.

So she said, 'Ryan dear, I appreciate your good intentions, at the moment that is, because I haven't had time to assess your ulterior motive. But don't you *dare* give my address to anyone ever again!'

'I won't,' he promised with a tinge of guilt. 'Did you . . . are you . . . I mean . . ?'

'No, I didn't, yes, I am, and if you mean what I think you mean, no, it's a purely business relationship. He's writing a book and he wants someone to help him research it and get it into some kind of order.'

'Oh—ho!' said Ryan, taking heart. 'So that's how the milk got into the coconut! I mean, the game has a new name now, does it?' He winked at her.

'You're incorrigible, Ryan,' she said acidly. 'I . . . I can't help visualising your future. There's nothing more disgusting than men who have never got over the bottom-pinching syndrome of their youth. I suspect you might be one of them.'

'And he won't? This Steven Harrow?'

'I wouldn't know,' she said coldly.

'Well, I'll tell *you* something for nothing, Morgan,' said Ryan irately and rather fast as a client entered the office and hesitated between the two desks, 'my uncle happens to be a church deacon and a solid pillar of society, not to mention a vice-president of that bank across the road . . . Good afternoon! May I help you, madam?' he enquired solicitously of the large lady on the other side of his desk. 'Won't you have a seat?' he invited, and turned back to Morgan as the lady sat, settling several large handbags, an umbrella and two parcels, no mean feat of dexterity. '. . . And it's his considered opinion that the urge to pinch a bottom or two is irresistible to men of all ages, and while it should be firmly controlled naturally, the odd outbreak whether you should be sixteen or sixty is not a moral sin but simply a momentary lapse in the face of almost unbearable temptation! So there!'

It was not the face of temptation that intrigued Morgan at that moment but the stunned face of the large lady across Ryan's desk, which had assumed an unattractive hue as she hastily regathered all her paraphernalia.

'Well, really,' she uttered as she staggered to her feet. 'I mean, really! I only came in to buy a ticket on the Sunlander to get to Bundaberg . . . the trouble with you young people is you have no respect! None at all! But I can tell you one thing, sonny, you try and lay your pinching hands about me and you'll get the quickest clip on the ear, mate, you've ever had!' She set a truculent course for the door, but added over her shoulder, 'That's the trouble with all you youngsters these days! Your parents didn't just realise the value of a good swift clip on the ear or a hearty kick in the pants. I tell you, I raised seven kids on it. . . .'

The smart closing of the glass door muffled the rest of her statement, but Morgan was already doubled up in silent laughter which Ryan's incredulous look didn't help to ease.

'Oh,' she gasped at last, wiping her eyes, 'that'll teach you, Ryan!'

'Do you think she'll write in and complain about me?' he asked gloomily.

'I don't know,' Morgan said callously, her sides still heaving with laughter. 'You might be forced to seek help from your advice-dispensing uncle across the road. They might need a juniour clerk.'

Ryan brightened. 'Of course! I only have to explain it all to Uncle Martin. You see, his bank is a shareholder in this travel agency.'

'Now that,' said Morgan after a moment, 'is what I would really call how the milk got into the coconut! *Since* we're looking for new names for old games. Like bottom-pinching lechery or . . . nepotism?'

'You have a nasty mind and a nasty tongue, Morgan,' Ryan said primly, but as his eyes caught hers he had to grin, reluctantly at first, and then they both burst into peals of laughter.

Come Saturday morning, though, and Morgan found she was feeling a lot less amused.

She inspected her wardrobe and finally chose a no-nonsense outfit that unfortunately, had she but realised it, emphasised her curves and her slimness in all the right places. It was a shirtwaister dress with long sleeves and a tiny revers collar, severely plain except for the colour which was an unusual shade of lime green. She wore no jewellery apart from her gold ring and bangle and a pair of medium-heeled court shoes in black patent.

But when she took one last look at herself in the mirror she was tempted to rip the whole outfit off and shrug into a pair of jeans. After all, it is Saturday, she thought rebelliously. And yet looking cool, calm and sophisticated does give me confidence, now doesn't it?

Yes, it does, she decided, and impatiently snatched up her slim patent leather purse.

'Where ya off to, Morgan?' one of the neighbours' children called as she reversed the Mini out of the garage. 'You're sure all done up!'

She hesitated again, but then determinedly put the car into first gear. 'Wouldn't be a bad idea if you did yourself up occasionally, Brad,' she called back with an airy wave, knowing that Brad's mother alternated between despair and laughter at her teenage son's ideas on suitable attire.

But Brad's words remained obstinately with her right until she stepped out of the Mini again beneath Steve Harrow's wooden decking. And when Steve himself opened his green front door for her and whistled admiringly, she blushed like an idiot.

'Come in, my pretty maid,' he said urbanely with a sweeping gesture. Then he rubbed his chin ruefully and tried to pat his wild hair into some sort of order. 'You caught me on the hop,' he added with a grin. 'In a word, I've just arisen from my couch.'

'So I see,' she said tartly as she preceded him up the spiral, internal staircase. 'We did say ten o'clock, didn't we? Because it's that right now. I hope you don't think I'm going to sit around and wait while you get dressed, etc., etc. At least,' she amended, 'I hope you realise you're going to pay me if I have to.'

'If I didn't, I do now,' Steve returned wryly as they stepped into the lounge. 'Are you the kind of person who doesn't sparkle until night-time, Morgan?' he asked as he took a purposeful grip of her arm and led her to a chair. 'Do sit down,' he added. 'I've just made some coffee. Will you have a cup? On the understanding, naturally, that you're being paid to drink it?' he queried softly but with the light of battle in his eyes.

Morgan tightened her lips. If I had any sense I'd get

up and run, she thought, but instead she retreated a little. 'Thank you, I'd like that,' she said politely. She sat down gracefully with her bag placed neatly beside her neat shoes and folded her hands in her lap. She looked up expectantly at him and some hidden compartment of her mind filed his shirtless image away with its smooth golden skin and wide strong shoulders, for all he wore was the inevitable slightly faded pair of jeans.

And some other part of her mind over which she had just as little control on occasions made her say, 'You've explained to me about cars and your reluctance to own one, but what is it you have about clothes?' quite conversationally but nonetheless with a barely concealed barb of sarcasm and distaste for his shirtless, shoeless state.

'None of the inhibitions you have, Morgan,' he said roughly. 'You know, I've met plenty of women and my fair share of tarts too, but your acid tongue takes the prize. I'd rather deal with a warmhearted slut than a cold, sharp-tongued bitch like you—certainly so early in the morning.' He turned abruptly and went into the kitchen.

It was sheer surprise that kept Morgan rooted to her chair. Her next reaction was hot, tearful anger, but as she dashed at her cheek two other thoughts struck her. Was her mascara as waterproof as the makers claimed, and the second, rather timidly, was that perhaps she'd deserved his ire?

But she set her chin resolutely at this treacherous thought. If Steve really thought she was as he'd described her, might it not make their relationship a whole lot easier?

He presented her with a cup of coffee in silence. She accepted it in silence and beyond one flickering glance which he did not meet, she felt as if she was now dealing with a mechanical robot. He left her to drink it without a word and presently she heard the shower gushing.

She took her cup and wandered out on to the deck. It was a perfect Brisbane autumn day, warm now but without the sultry humidity of high summer that made life in this corner of the world a bit of a trial—unless you happened to have been born and bred farther north—and the sky was a deep cloudless blue. But the city itself, towards the horizon wore a smudged, rather blurred outline today, a testimony to the fact that Brisbane, although referred to often by southerners a little scathingly as a big 'country town', had its problems with pollution and a climatic set of conditions that didn't allow it to disperse easily.

As I well recall, Morgan thought, from my geography lectures. She grimaced slightly and looked around the wooden deck with its yellow canvas chairs and colourful plant baskets hanging from the overlapping roof that covered about half the area of it. I was quite happy with my little flat until I saw this, she thought, too. Quite happy. . . .

She shook herself and stepped indoors into the study, to find Steve there already dressed in fresh clothes and with his hair still damp from the shower.

'There you are,' he said casually, but the quick penetrating glance he gave her showed her that his blue eyes were were still cold and distant. She repressed a slight shiver.

'Look,' he went on, 'do you think you can concentrate in here with me bashing away at the typewriter at the same time? Because if not I can set up a table in the lounge for you.'

'I don't mind,' she answered quietly. 'Perhaps *you* might find it difficult to concentrate—with someone else in the room.' She looked around and noted the new table and chair in one corner, also another typewriter.

He shrugged. 'You might be right. Actually, I think it's easier if I move out into the lounge. You're more liable to need the reference books at this stage. Can you give me a hand? I'll take the small table out.'

Between them they moved a table, chair and the type-writer into the lounge.

She stood back and viewed the arrangement uncertainly. 'Are you sure you want to be in here?' she asked.

'I don't mind where I am when I write,' he said coolly, 'so long as it's peaceful.'

'Very well,' she said steadily, and put down a ream of paper and a box of carbon beside the typewriter. 'What do you want me to do this morning?'

'This.' He led the way back into the study, where he placed a wire basket in her hands that was full to over-flowing. 'I haven't even sorted the the copies from the original. You can do that, and you can correct the typing errors and if you come across anything incomprehensible, I mean grammatically or otherwise, make a note of it and we can go through it together later. Some of it might need retyping. You can do that for me.'

Morgan worked steadily for the next three hours to the accompaniment of the typewriter next door. At times it thundered as if Steve was trying to drive the keys through the table and at other times it stopped abruptly, either to resume tentatively or with machinegun rapidity. The only time she broke off her own work was when the machine had been idle for a good ten minutes and a low mutter of curses rose and echoed around the house with a wide-ranging fluency.

She hesitated, then stepped into the lounge to see her employer with a tangle of typing ribbon in his lap and black fingermarks all over the machine—and a wild look in his eyes.

'Let me,' she offered, and firmly pushed him out of the way. He strode out on to the deck, pulling his hands through his hair as if he'd like to tear it all out.

It took Morgan ten minutes to untangle the mess and

put in a new ribbon. Then she cleaned up the machine and indicated to her employer that all was well again.

He stopped pacing the deck like a caged lion. 'I don't understand it!' he said, still looking grim. 'I can build a house, I can excavate middens, I can do a whole lot of things that require patience and dexterity. Why the hell can't I ever change a typewriter ribbon without getting all tied up in it?'

'Why don't you wash your hands?' she said soothingly. 'It's all set to go now.'

He looked down at his black hands and the pinched white look around his mouth receded a little. He even smiled faintly. 'Thanks,' he said offhandedly, 'I will.'

At two o'clock though, the pangs of hunger Morgan was experiencing became acute. She stood up and pushed her work away resolutely. The typewriter was still going hammer and tongs next door.

'But,' she murmured to herself, '*I* don't have to starve myself.'

The kitchen was dim and cool and the refrigerator surprisingly well stocked. She made ham and salad sandwiches and a pot of coffee, marvelling as she did at Steve Harrow's versatility. For the delicious, crusty bread she found in the breadbox was very fresh and obviously home-made. Unless she thought, he had a bread-baking neighbour in these parts.

She unobtrusively placed a plate of sandwiches and a cup of coffee beside Steve's elbow and left the lounge almost immediately as he nodded absently but didn't look up.

She ate her own lunch at her desk and rinsed her dishes, but didn't go into the lounge again but got straight back to work.

Truth to tell, the more she read of his book, the more fascinated she became. It was basically a story of murder and suspense, but the strength of the characters he wrote about seemed almost to overshadow the plot.

The central pivot of the story was a brilliant scientist who alternated between being an absentminded boffin who could never remember what day it was and a high-living bachelor who could never remember who his current girl-friend was. Until four of those ladies, impressed by his incurable generosity, even when he called them by the wrong names, banded together to form a union and by subtle and hilarious means managed to, as one of them put it laconically, 'Keep the action here—right here with us four. After all, when you're on to a good thing as we are, why share it around any further? So long as he gets a bit of variety he doesn't really know whether he's with Helen of Troy or the Queen of Sheba!'

But when the scientist was accused of murdering a colleague in order to steal a secret formula, the ladies found that their union was pressed into more urgent action than merely keeping other females at bay. They all turned detective.

Morgan found she hadn't been able to resist skimming through the hundred or so pages of manuscript to get the gist of the plot before settling down to the corrections. But fascinating and funny as she found it, she also found it disturbed her slightly for the insight into the psyche of the human female Steve Harrow displayed in his portrayal of the four women, and the way he had of making each one of them likeable and real despite their slightly strange sense of morals even this early in the book.

And she wondered as she wielded liquid paper and pen to correct his erratic typing which one of them he would choose finally for the scientist, because that seemed to be the way the book was heading.

She was so engrossed, in fact, that she didn't realise that four o'clock had come and gone until she became suddenly conscious of the silence and the lengthening shadows on the deck outside. A movement at the doorway made her turn quickly to see him standing at the doorway contemplating her thoughtfully.

She blinked and closed her eyes briefly to make sure she wasn't dreaming. But when she opened them again he was still there, dressed in a dark suit with a pale blue silk shirt and his hair tamed into some sort of order.

She felt her mouth fall open and shut it with a click. Then she glanced at her watch and gasped. It was five o'clock.

'Oh dear,' she said ruefully. 'I had no idea! I'm afraid I'm only about halfway through this lot. Why didn't you tell me it was so late?'

'You seemed lost to the world,' said Steve with a wry grin. 'Besides, it's an extra five dollars for you and I thought you were as well occupied doing that as anything else while you waited for me. You see,' he added to her look of bewilderment, 'I also thought you wouldn't mind giving me a lift into town now.'

'I . . . well, no.' She stood up and tidied the desk as she spoke. 'But how will you get back?' she asked, and could have bitten her tongue. What did she care how he got back?

'I'm not coming back tonight. Shall we go?'

'O.K.,' she said a little dazedly and picked up her purse. Why do I feel let down somehow? she asked herself as he closed the louvred doors. As if I'm being summarily dismissed like a schoolchild?

Because you're mad, Morgan, that's why!

She stiffened her spine as he turned back to her and led the way down the spiral staircase.

Steve didn't talk much on the drive into town and she found herself wishing fervently and crazily that he'd say something argumentative, even something that annoyed her, rather than this cool virtual dismissal of her presence.

After all, she thought angrily, he's using me! At least, using my car.

She said tartly as she approached the Normanby five-ways, 'Where do you want to go?'

'Er . . . Lennon's,' he answered mildly. 'But anywhere around here will do. I can take a cab.'

'It's a little late,' she pointed out acidly. 'I'm in the wrong lane now to be letting you off.'

'So you are,' he commented dryly as she was inexorably shepherded by the traffic towards the city centre and away from Herston.

Morgan gritted her teeth and didn't say another word until she had reached Queen Street and the imposing façade of Lennon's Hotel.

She brought the car to a halt in a no-standing zone behind a silver Rolls-Royce and turned to him. 'There. Is this close enough, sir?'

'Oh yes,' he said with a slight quiver in his voice, 'this is fine. Thank you, Glamorgan.' He opened the door and stepped out. 'I'll see you next week, shall I?' He half turned and waved to a group of well dressed people standing on the steps, then turned back to her and extracted several notes from his pocket. 'Your wages, ma'am,' he said silkily, and put the notes down on the seat. 'Together with a little tip for your gracious . . . lift,' he added contemptuously.

Morgan reached across for the money with the express intention of flinging it in his face, but he reached in and grasped her wrist as if guessing her intention. Their eyes clashed and then Morgan's shifted slightly and took in the girl who had come to stand behind him—an exquisitely gowned creature with pale gold hair and pouting lips. The girl was staring at the money in Morgan's hand with a dawning expression of bewilderment.

'Put it in your purse, Morgan,' Steve ordered. 'After all, it is for services rendered, isn't it?'

The girl behind put out a tentative hand and said uncertainly, 'Steve?' She bent a little so that she could see fully into the car, and her eyes widened as they fell on Morgan. 'Who is this, Steve?' she asked.

He straightened and turned. 'Why, Sheila,' he said, 'I didn't hear you come up. This is my secretary-cum-chauffeur.' He waved towards Morgan. 'When she's not my chief tormentor, that is. I must say you're looking gorgeous tonight, darling,' he added warmly.

Morgan took a furious breath. 'Would you please close the door,' she demanded icily, and jumped as the door was unexpectedly slammed shut and a pair of impatient knuckles drummed on the roof.

She jammed the car into gear and shot out into the traffic, causing minor havoc behind her, and the last glimpse she got of the pair of them showed Sheila wearing an expression of pained surprise and Steve laughing.

'Oh!' she exclaimed aloud as forcefully as she could, and beat the steering wheel with her fist. 'I hate him! I thought I hated my father, but it was *nothing* compared to this. And the same to you!' she called to the driver who had pulled up beside her at a set of red lights and was expressing a whole lot of pent-up emotion about women drivers, particularly ones in yellow Minis who pulled out right under your wheels.

Fortunately before the exchange could become any more acrimonious the lights changed, and although the other driver visibly debated with himself whether to follow Morgan, his wife who had sat in the middle of the slanging match prevailed upon him to take a right turning as Morgan shot on straight ahead.

Not that Morgan would have cared which way he went, and her magnificent bout of temper stayed with her all the way home.

It was only after she had had a cup of tea that she found herself calming down, to feel utterly drained and miserable. She had a warm bath and a light supper which she picked at uninterestedly and finally pushed away almost untasted.

She tried to watch television, but found that she couldn't concentrate, so she went to bed, to toss and turn and re-run the day's events through her tired brain like a video tape, over and over again.

Maybe I was in the wrong, she thought miserably several times. Maybe I started out on the wrong foot this morning. So much so that I managed to kill all his good humour stone dead. For ever.

She sat up amidst the twisted bedclothes and sighed deeply. 'All right,' she admitted to the darkness, 'but when he's good-humoured, he's also insidiously trying to get me to go to bed with him, I know! So that he can prove this theory that all men have—that *all* women without a man of one kind or another are dead and dried up and denying the very reason for their existence.'

What a load of poppycock, she thought contemptuously. As I very well know. If anything, nine times out of ten it's an invitation to disaster. Just take his four women in his book. O.K., so he might be able to make them live and breathe, but what can he really know of their pain and sense of futility when they're no longer young and beautiful? Or when they've been spurned by some man.

And I imagine there might be a few whom he himself has spurned. But not me. She lay back and pulled out and polished a little, as yet unspoken dream she'd dreamed from time to time. Not a real dream, more in the nature of a daydream. Of herself going into politics and becoming a Member of Parliament. Preferably Federal Parliament, because it seemed to offer wider vistas, but State Parliament was not to be spurned, especially as Queensland was becoming more and more a sort of focal point within the Commonwealth, a state incredibly rich in mineral resources.

She lay there and felt the soothing wash of this day-dream play over her heated emotions. Yes, state politics were not to be ignored, despite the fact that Queensland was regarded as something of a joke by its more sophisticated southern neighbours, as a state where things moved more slowly—this trend generally attributed to the balmy climate—and it was often cuttingly referred to as the 'deep north' and its population referred to with a mixture of affection and sarcasm as 'banana benders'. And yet ever-increasing hordes of southerners were flocking to Queensland to soak up the sunshine on their vacations and to retire to it.

Morgan sighed again and abandoned herself to the intoxicating thought of being 'somebody' one day. But just as she was drifting off to sleep, she was struck by an uncomfortable thought of a more immediate nature. Should she go back next Saturday? Or should she attempt to cut the connection once more?

And the last coherent thought she had was that it might not need any cutting on her part at all.

Sunday dawned cloudy and dull, a sullen kind of a day that held more than a hint of winter.

Morgan donned a pair of workmanlike overalls and displayed a boldly written DO NOT DISTURB sign on her front door which was a rarely evoked treaty she had evolved with the neighbouring children, who tended to treat her flat like a common 'get away from Mum and family' meeting ground.

Not that she normally objected to this, but on the odd occasion she found she did need a barrier against her flat becoming like the Roma Street Forum.

However, she didn't realise that on the very few times she put the sign up, she also evoked a sense of consternation down the length of the street as to her well-being that caused many a mum and child to gossip avidly for hours.

'That's him!' Brad Smith averred from on top of his gatepost as a tall fair man turned into the driveway of Morgan's block of flats. 'I tell you,' he added to his crowd of younger admirers, not unconscious of his position of leading 'hoon' of the neighbourhood and therefore the attendant burden of being the very personification of wisdom, 'I tell you, she hasn't been the same since he last visited her!'

Morgan was vacuuming vigorously when the doorbell rang. She ignored it twice and then stormed to the door. 'Can't you read?' she demanded angrily as she flung it open. 'Oh! It's you!' She coloured and then frowned as she glimpsed several young heads peeping round odd corners and caught the sound of a stifled giggle.

'It is indeed I,' Steve Harrow offered gravely. 'Can I come in?'

'Why . . . I mean, what for?' she asked disjointedly. 'The place is a mess. . . .'

'Because I want to kiss you,' he said politely, his blue eyes sparkling with amusement. 'I thought you might prefer it to be . . . er . . . more private, but if you don't mind the audience, who am I to complain, eh, fellows?' he said a little louder and with a jerk of his head that caused Brad Smith to fall off the low parapet he was balancing on, just out of Morgan's range of vision, into the shrubbery.

'You . . . you're impossible!' she breathed as he stepped forward as if to take her into his arms. 'No! Oh, all right, come in,' she said furiously, and closed the door with something of a snap for the benefit of the gallery.

'You do realise,' she went on coldly as she stood with her back to the door, 'that you've probably set the whole street gossiping about me now, don't you?'

Steve grinned. 'Dear Morgan, I'm sure that's nothing new. A gorgeous girl like yourself is always food for gossip.'

She narrowed her eyes and stared at him. He had on the same blue silk shirt, but the collar was open now and the sleeves rolled untidily halfway up his forearms, and he had his jacket and tie slung over one arm and his hands pushed into his hip pockets. He looked a little tired, she thought inconsequently.

But she said warily, 'All right! Let's not go into that now. What do you want? I'm not driving you out to Mount Nebo today, so. . . .'

She didn't finish her sentence because he dropped his jacket and tie carelessly and moved deliberately towards her.

'I told you what I came for, Morgan,' he drawled, and reached out a hand to pin her gently to the door as she tried to sidestep him.

Her heart jumped into her throat and her limbs started to tremble as if possessed of a life of their own. She licked her lips and stared up into his face so close to her own now, and felt as if she was drowning in his sombre, heavy-lidded gaze.

He brought his other hand up and traced the outline of her lips with one finger. 'Do you know what your mouth reminds me of, Morgan?' he asked so quietly that she barely heard him. 'Like some ripe beautiful fruit ready to be plundered. And your skin, so pale and perfect, also offers its own intrinsic invitation to plunder and ravishment. It makes me want to touch it and bruise it. . . .' He lowered his head as he spoke and drew her into the circle of his arms. 'Like this,' he said huskily, his last words before his mouth descended on hers, gently and delicately teasing her own frozen lips apart and making her whole body come throbbingly alive as he moulded her with his arms to the hard powerful length of him.

It was a long exploratory kiss, not hurtful as he'd done it on the night he'd hijacked her, as Ryan had called it, but as if drinking deeply of some powerful, intoxicating essence, and Morgan found that for the life of her she didn't have the will to resist, didn't have the will to do anything but savour the unfamiliar sensations of her body.

And when it ended finally she dropped her head to his shoulder for a long moment.

'Why . . . why did you do that?' she whispered shakily into his shirt, and for a brief instant found herself wishing powerfully that there was no silk shirt there so that she could move her lips along his bare skin. She made a determined effort and pushed herself away from him with both hands on his hard, muscled chest to stare up at him.

He loosened the circle of his arms, but instead of releasing her, picked her up and carried her through to the lounge to deposit her carefully into a chair.

She gazed up at him wordlessly but with troubled, desolate eyes. Steve returned her look, but his own blue, blue eyes were curiously expressionless. Then he lifted his shoulders in a disclaiming gesture and cast himself down on to the settee.

He ran a hand through his untidy hair. 'Why did I do it?' he said lightly. 'Because you looked so cross, because I felt like it as I said, and also,' he hesitated and shot her keen glance, 'also to apologise for being such a grouch yesterday.'

Morgan felt her eyes widen incredulously.

'*Also*,' Steve added with an imp of laughter tugging at his lips, 'I was a little relieved to see you all in one piece this morning. I had this disturbing vision last night of you driving yourself up a tree out of sheer anger and frustration.'

She blushed hotly then as she recalled some of the things she'd said to the man in the car beside her at the traffic lights—out of sheer rage and frustration.

Steve Harrow's whole face came alive with amusement

and he raised his eyebrows quizzically as he took in her hot cheeks and clenched hands.

'Don't tell me you did?' he demanded with a grin.

'Of course not! I . . . oh, it doesn't matter,' she said crossly. 'I was angry,' she admitted with a wry look. 'And . . . well, since we're on the subject,' she added haltingly, 'perhaps I should apologise too. I sometimes—well, you're not the only person who thinks I have a nasty mind and a nasty tongue,' she went on hastily, with a vivid picture of Ryan in her mind's eye. 'I shall try to curb it in future,' she said stiffly. 'That is, if you promise. . . .' She stopped abruptly.

'Promise not to kiss you again?' he prompted lazily. 'You didn't seem to mind too much at the time, Morgan,' he added softly.

'Because you caught me unawares,' she said tartly, and not altogether truthfully. 'All right,' she added steadily to his ironic look, 'we've proved I'm not a block of wood. I didn't fight and I didn't die of revulsion. And since I'm being so truthful, why don't you admit that's exactly why you did it? To prove something to me? But even you must admit one kiss doesn't make a . . . make a. . . .'

'Make a summer,' he supplied. 'Not at all, but since we're mixing our metaphors why shouldn't we admit that even swallows refuse to stay out in the cold for ever?'

She took a deep breath. 'I know you think I'm out in the cold, I know you think I don't . . . *can't* realise it until I've experienced . . . your brand of warmth. I also know that you're wrong about me. Look,' she said urgently, 'although I didn't think I would, I really feel I'm going to enjoy helping you with your book. Why can't we just leave it at that?' Her voice rose fractionally.

He stood up and said casually, 'When you work that one out, Morgan, you might understand the rest.' He looked around for his jacket and bent to pick it up. 'By the way, I'm having a small party next Saturday evening.

Only about twenty people, but most of them rather interesting. Why don't you bring some glad rags with you so that you can change when you've finished work and join us?' He turned to the door. 'Until then, Glamorgan,' he said over his shoulder, and was gone before she had a chance to marshall her startled wits.

CHAPTER FIVE

'THAT's it!' Morgan said to herself. It was mid-week and she sat at her desk shuffling a selection of air, coach and rail tickets into a plastic envelope bearing the agency's name embossed in gold on it.

'Done,' she added to Ryan, who had cocked a semi-interested ear in her direction. 'And only to be undone, altered or changed in any way over my dead body!'

'Very wise,' Ryan commented. 'Just make sure you tell Mr Wallace your feelings on the subject. If you ask me, the old boy gets a kick out of your company ...' He broke off and whistled beneath his breath. 'Talking of bodies, Morgan,' he said out of the side of his mouth, 'check this one, will you?'

Morgan lifted her eyes to the door and her busy fingers froze. It was indeed a superbly feminine form entering the agency. It was also the form of the girl Steve Harrow had joined at Lennons' on the previous Saturday, the girl he'd called Sheila.

Morgan felt her eyes widen as the full impact of this girl hit her. She had been reluctantly impressed despite her supreme irritation on Saturday evening. But now, as the girl swung across the office with a gliding walk that was both sensuous and riveting, she felt herself doing a mental double take. A swift glance from the corner of her eye revealed that Ryan was as impressed if not more so. In fact his eyes were bulging visibly.

The girl stopped before the two desks and her pale blue eyes flickered from Morgan to Ryan and then back to Morgan, and a tiny frown sprang to her smooth

76

forehead beneath her wheat-gold, magnificently careless coiffure.

Morgan swallowed, and when her telephone rang just then beside her she plucked up the receiver as if snatching at a lifeline, while the girl turned to Ryan but still with a look of speculation in her eyes.

It was a curious telephone conversation Morgan conducted. One part of her mind was assimilating the pale lavender, clinging crêpe dress Sheila wore, demurely styled yet clinging to and emphasising her figure and trying to hear what she was saying to Ryan—and the other half attempting to talk into the phone at the same time.

'Yes, madam,' she said into the phone. 'There are a number of companies that run a daily coach service to Sydney.'

'. . . Lord Howe Island for two,' she heard Sheila say to Ryan. 'I thought it would be a perfect place to spend a long weekend.'

Perfect, Morgan thought, having been to Lord Howe Island herself. Especially perfect to share it with a lover.

She felt herself colour faintly and said hastily into the phone, 'Cairns? And Cooktown? I'm so sorry, madam, I must have misheard you. I thought you said Sydney. Yes, indeed . . .'

She put down the phone just as Sheila rose gracefully, and for a moment their eyes met. The other girl still looked puzzled and was about to say something to Morgan when another client, in the form of Mr Wallace, trod the deep pile of the carpet towards Morgan.

She greeted him gratefully and Sheila turned back to Ryan with a lift of her perfect eyebrows.

And by the time Morgan had talked Mr Wallace out of 'just one little—very minor change really' and bade him farewell and happy landings most heartily, Sheila had left.

Morgan sat back and looked at Ryan from beneath her lashes. He was still wearing a totally bemused expression and even sniffing gently.

'Chanel?' he said finally. 'Number Five or Twenty-one?'

'Arpège,' Morgan said prosaically.

'The perfume of the gods anyway,' Ryan said dreamily. 'He's a lucky guy!' He shook his head and sighed deeply.

'Who?' Morgan was careful to sound casual.

'The guy Miss Somerville is planning to have a lost weekend with on Lord Howe . . . Oh, that it were me—I mean I! What I mean is, Ryan Clarke, if you know what I mean.'

Morgan couldn't help giggling at his uplifted yet mournful expression. 'Challenge him to a duel,' she said flippantly, and discovered curiously that she felt like crying.

'I would,' Ryan said promptly. 'Only I don't know his name.'

'So she hasn't made any bookings yet?'

'No. She was just doing the groundwork, I'd say.'

'Perhaps it's her husband she's taking?'

'No!' Ryan protested on a note of anguish. And then, less dramatically, 'No—I checked that out. No rings. No wedding or engagement rings anyway. Hey, do you know her, Morgan?' he added hopefully.

Morgan shrugged. 'No. Why should I?'

'I don't know. Just seemed to me she kept looking at you as if she was trying to work out where she'd seen you before.'

'Probably mixed me up with someone else,' Morgan said calmly and wondered why she found it necessary to lie.

And by the time Friday came round she still hadn't

worked that one out or come to a decision about whether
she should stay for Steve Harrow's party the following
evening. She recalled his last words—when you work that
one out, Morgan. . . . She sighed exasperatedly and
massaged her temples with her fingertips. It had been a
long, busy day this Friday too.

She looked up and caught Ryan eyeing her. 'What is
it?' she queried.

'You look as if you could do with a drink, Morgan.
Dare I offer to buy you one when we close, or will I get
my head bitten off?'

Morgan smiled feebly. 'Your offer would be very gratefully received,' she said meekly, and even managed to
raise a laugh as he pretended to fall off his chair.

'My, my!' he said half an hour later when they were
both seated in a dim, intimate lounge bar in a posh city
hotel, 'I feel I should pinch myself.' He sobered.
'Morgan—friend—are you going to tell me what's been
bugging you lately? You know it does help to talk things
out sometimes.'

She fiddled with her paper mat and started to speak
several times, then shrugged helplessly.

'How about, if I set the ball rolling, then?' he said
lightly. 'I know it's Steve Harrow. What I don't
know is why he should be such a problem. I mean,
what more could you want in a man? He's made his
own way in a tough field—I know that because I
have another uncle who's an academic—in fact,
everything about him seems to point to his eligibility!'

Morgan sipped her drink thoughtfully and wondered
briefly what Ryan would say if he knew who it was Sheila
Somerville was planning to take to Lord Howe Island.
But then I don't *know* that, she reminded herself. I'm only
guessing. And she hasn't been back yet to make the bookings. But I have this feeling . . .

She sipped her drink thoughtfully beneath Ryan's relentless scrutiny and for some strange reason felt an overwhelming urge to bare her soul. She said, 'I don't deny his eligibility . . . oh, look, how would you feel, Ryan, if you met someone that you liked above all else—say someone like Miss Somerfield—but she didn't reciprocate and then something happened to make her feel morally responsible for you. Felt she had a duty towards you. And that's all she felt. How would *you* feel?'

Ryan blinked. 'I might go out and cut my throat . . . No! Hang on, you got me sidetracked. Do you mean he feels that way about you or you about him?' he asked on a note of fascination.

'Him about me,' she said ruefully, and rubbed her face. 'Complicated by the fact that he's a man.'

'I don't get the last bit.'

'You should,' she said tartly. 'I mean, who's been mooning around the office for the past couple of days on the strength of a ten-minute meeting with a blonde bombshell? I mean, men have certain urges . . . don't they?' she added a little uncertainly.

'Oh, they do that,' Ryan said happily. Then he narrowed his eyes. 'I don't know if I read you right, but are you trying to say women don't?' he queried acutely.

'No—o. . . . Oh, God! I don't know what I'm trying to say!' Morgan pushed her drink round in a tight circle distractedly.

'Morgan,' he said slowly, 'you told me once that there's nothing more disgusting than lecherous old men. *I* think there's nothing more pathetic than the thought of you living and dying an old maid. No, don't interrupt,' he said quietly as she moved restlessly. 'On this matter of Steve Harrow you're working from two unsound assumptions. One is that it's a purely physical attraction for him, but you can't *know* that unless you subscribe to the theory that only women are capable of deeper feeling. Do you?'

'I . . . no, not really.'

'You don't sound too sure about it, kid,' he said with a grin, but sobered almost immediately. 'The other unsound assumption you're making is that if you did give in to him, which I rather gather one part of you wants to, and if it doesn't end in wedding bells and all the trimmings, you'll be quite destroyed.'

She was silent.

'But that's the most unsound assumption of the two,' Ryan went on gently, 'if anything. So you might take a knock, get clobbered perhaps. Growing mentally can be painful. But even that's preferable to being retarded.' He shrugged. 'You'd be horrified at the thought of growing up without learning to read and write, wouldn't you?'

She smiled a little tearfully. 'I don't know if that's a fair equation. But it seems to be a peculiarly *male* argument. Which makes me wonder if it isn't easier for men to . . . get clobbered and bounce right back.'

'It shouldn't be, not these days, Morgan. Women have science on their side now. You can avoid getting pregnant and you also have a militant sisterhood that's campaigned long and hard to have the stigma removed from illegitimacy anyway. Speaking broadly, you're as free as any man to experiment if you wish. Why should it be harder to bounce back? Unless you're trying to tell me,' he added with a wicked twinkle in his eye, 'that all this progress women have made is worth nothing? That you'd rather be back in the good old days when society had very rigid rules to protect women from themselves and the consequences of their folly?'

'Ryan . . .' she put her head to one side, 'you should have been a lawyer!'

'I know,' he grinned. 'Although I must admit I'm speaking on a subject that's very close to my heart.'

'I can imagine,' she drawled. 'You're a walking, talking advertisement for promiscuity, in fact.'

'Now there I disagree. In fact I'm a great fan of Women's Lib—genuinely! Because I happen to like women and think they got the thin end of the wedge for too long, and secondly because it adds a lot of spice to the game. The dear little things don't fall into your arms any more like ripe plums. They can afford to be mighty choosy. It kinda puts one on one's mettle, if you know what I mean.'

'Oh, Ryan,' she said laughingly, 'you're impossible, really!'

He leant forward. 'But I made you laugh, didn't I? That's the first time you've really smiled for days.' He covered her hand with his own and pressed it gently.

'You did too,' she said gratefully. 'I'm sorry I've been so painful.'

'That's O.K.,' he said cheerfully. 'Er ... since we're on the subject can I offer you one last piece of advice?'

She nodded wryly.

'It's something I read that stuck in my mind—yes, I do read, Morgan—and it was written by a woman, actually Dorothy Sayers. I don't know if you've read any of hers—anyway, she said that the only sin passion can commit is to be joyless. If you can't lie down laughing, you shouldn't lie down at all.'

Morgan took an involuntary breath that jolted her and she marvelled again at the unexpected depths there were to Ryan. But she said lightly, 'And in your own short but active career, have you found that a good keystone to work from?'

'The best,' he assured her solemnly. Then, 'Heavens! Enough of this deep stuff. If I promise not take any liberties why don't we partake of the delicious smorgasbord they're offering over there? I could eat a horse!'

On the strength of Ryan's little homily, Morgan washed her hair later that night and decided for once and for all that she would go the party. But the next morning as she drove steadily westward, Ryan's advice wasn't quite as comforting as it had been.

'After all,' she said to herself, 'I can't picture myself saying to Steve Harrow this morning—look, take me to bed, we both seem to want it, so let's give it a try and forget about analysing it all! Now can I?'

But as she turned into his driveway she had made a resolve to at least try and relax and not be so prickly. She nosed the car under the deck, then took a sudden deep breath. For there was already a car parked there, a brilliant emerald green Porsche.

'I wonder,' she murmured to herself, and felt a strange prickle of intuition.

She didn't have to wonder long, because when the front door opened it was Sheila Somerville who stood there.

'Miss Jones,' Sheila said brightly. She stopped and narrowed her blue eyes. 'Of course! I knew I'd seen you before. You're the girl from the travel agency, aren't you? Do come in. Steve asked me to let you in. He's cooking,' she added with a conspiratorial wink.

'Oh,' said Miss Jones. 'Thank you.' She followed Sheila's neat pert rear, which was displayed to maximum advantage in a pair of tight, slinky raw silk trousers, up the staircase.

At the top Sheila turned back and said charmingly, 'I'm Sheila Somerville. Steven's told me about you. And

I *knew* I'd seen you somewhere before. Oh, by the way,' she put a hand on Morgan's arm and said softly with engaging frankness, 'you won't mention anything about seeing me in your agency, will you? It's to be a surprise for Steve.' Her eyes sparkled and she resumed her normal voice. 'Yes,' she said again, 'he's told me *all* about you and what a clever little secretary you are, Miss Jones.'

Morgan blanched and thought, Dear God! I hope not all. . . .

She cleared her throat. 'Please call me Morgan.'

'What a quaint name,' Sheila murmured. 'I believe you're a new Australian?'

Morgan blinked. 'Am I? I was born here.'

'First generation, then,' Sheila amended. 'I always think that's still somewhat new. Silly of me, isn't it?' She laughed charmingly. 'But you see, my ancestors came over with the First Fleet.'

Morgan choked as the thrust of Sheila's sticky brand of sweetness suddenly hit home. 'Oh yes?' she replied interestedly. 'Do you mean your ancestors were convicts?'

The bright glowing façade Sheila Somerville was exhibiting slipped somewhat. 'Not at all,' she said coldly and with a flash of venom in her pale eyes. But it was all gone in an instant as she said briskly, 'I believe you're coming to the party. Wouldn't you like to come through and hang up your dress? I'll show you the way. Oh, Steve,' she called over her shoulder, 'your secretary-cum-chauffeur's here, darling! What shall I do with her?'

Steve emerged from the kitchen with his hair looking wilder than ever and a blue butcher's apron tied over his jeans. He took one look at Morgan's face and with a look of acute amusement, steered her into the study with a murmured word for Sheila and closed the door. 'Don't say it,' he warned. 'It comes of being born a Somerville. You might even get to like her when you get to know her better.'

Morgan opened her mouth to refute this hotly, but her earlier thoughts returned to sustain her. She shrugged and said mildly, 'Perhaps I will. Are you working today?'

'I doubt it,' he said wryly. 'I . . . er . . . hoped you wouldn't mind continuing what you did last week?'

'I don't mind,' she said equably. She put her purse down on the table. 'I'll hang my dress up. Not that it matters really, it's pretty uncrushable.'

'I'll do it.'

'No! No, I don't mind.' She turned away determinedly and opened the door.

'Morgan,' he said softly, 'I . . .'

'Don't mind me,' she said over her shoulder. 'I do know my way around, remember?'

It was his turn to shrug, but he followed her down the short passageway and stood leaning against the door frame as she entered the bedroom and stopped as if she'd been shot, with her heart beating suffocatingly.

For some reason Steve Harrow's bedroom hadn't been far from her mind ever since she had spent a night there. She had tried to tell herself that it had been the painting of the bush that had made such an impression on her, and the unfamilar but undeniably beautiful music he'd played for her. The symphony of colours and textures—velvet on wood, ruby on teak, bare skin on the finest cotton. . . .

But it had been none of these, she realised in that instant. It had been the underlying image of herself lying on that bed, undressed so that her skin gleamed pale on the violet sheet with her hair spread accross the pillow and her arms raised to welcome him in a gesture of wanton aban-don. . . .

She shut her eyes and half raised one hand as if to ward

off a painful blow. But she lowered her hand and opened her eyes just as quickly. Nothing had changed. The filmy peppermint green negligee was still lying on the unmade bed as if its owner had dropped it there carelessly. And a pair of fluffy matching high-heeled mules stood at the foot of the bed next to a discarded pyjama top which she recognised immediately, having worn it herself on that never-to-be-forgotten night.

Of course, she thought painfully, that's why *she* wanted me to come in here and *he* didn't. What a fool I am! Thank God he's standing behind me!

She forced herself to move forward steadily and prayed that her agonised reflections had taken no more than a few seconds as she walked into the dressing room.

She didn't linger once the dress was hung up and her case stored neatly, but she did dredge up every ounce of composure she possessed to steel herself for what seemed like an endless walk back across the room to where Steve still stood with his shoulders propped against the door-frame, his arms folded across his chest and his eyes narrowed as they probed her face.

She said the first thing that came to mind. 'Are you going to marry Peter off to Leonie?' Peter was the scientist in his book and Leonie one of the 'Gang of Four', as his lady loves laughingly called themselves. 'I must confess,' she went on brightly, 'I'm dying of curiosity. Have you written any more?'

His eyes flickered and she knew she'd thrown him momentarily and congratulated herself.

But he said smoothly, 'I have other plans for Leonie. As a non-sequitur though, that was faultless, Glamorgan. And yet I'm a little disappointed. I thought I might have rated more than that.'

Her feelings of self-congratulation acquired a tinge of deflation. I might have known I couldn't fool him, she thought bitterly. But really, I'm scarcely equipped to deal with this situation even as a crass outsider, let alone . . . let alone. . . . Her thoughts trailed off incoherently at that point.

She gathered herself and said seriously, 'I'm sorry, I shouldn't have intruded like that. I don't usually have to have things spelt out for me. Shall we . . . shall I get to work now? It gets pretty expensive—for you, I mean—to have to stand around chatting to me.'

Steve straightened and ran his hands through his hair. 'You have a marvellous line in put-downs, Morgan,' he said. 'I don't suppose there's any way we could discuss this? Any way I could get across that implacable barrier you've erected?'

I've erected! Morgan thought chokingly. Dear God! Surely even Ryan wouldn't expect to discuss a present lover with a prospective one? I may be a bit old-fashioned, but all the same . . . !

She said steadily, 'If I'd allowed you to hang up my dress there'd have been nothing to discuss, would there?'

'Wouldn't there?' he queried. 'That's an odd statement. In fact it's an assumption that I was trying to hide something from you.'

She trembled as an inner voice took her unawares. Who's hiding what from who? it asked unkindly.

Oh, nonsense, she replied to herself. Surely one's allowed some form of self-preservation? At least a measure of it?

'Look,' she said, 'perhaps I am old-fashioned, but it's embarrassing to walk into this kind of thing. That doesn't mean I'm censuring either of you, though. I . . . I. . . .'

'Aren't you, Morgan?' he asked deliberately. 'Do you mean you've forgotten how I kissed you last week?' He reached out and touched her lips deliberately with one finger. 'Don't you think it's strange that I should have done that and then gone to bed with Sheila last night? Isn't that a normal reaction?'

'I suppose it is,' she said coolly. 'I . . . yes, I did react like that for an instant.' My, my, she marvelled, how sane and level-headed I sound! If only I wasn't standing quite so close to him. . . . She stepped back a pace or two and to cover her leaping pulses ran her fingers through her hair and pushed it behind her ears.

Steve straightened. 'And what conclusion did you come to, Morgan? That I'm a sex-maniac?' he asked quietly.

'No,' she said nervously as he reached out again, this time to fiddle with the collar of her dress. She licked her lips and stared resolutely at the hollows at the base of his neck which were tantalisingly close. I wonder if Sheila has this overwhelming desire to lay her lips on his skin, she thought miserably. Perhaps she does. . . .

'What, then, Morgan?' he asked, and she felt his breath fan her forehead and his knuckles at the base of her throat and at the same time the actual physical sensation of her breasts swelling and her nipples hardening.

Oh God! she thought distractedly, and moved away from him determinedly. He didn't follow.

She said to the picture on the wall, with her fists clenching and unclenching consciously, 'It proved to me that although you sometimes might feel like . . . kissing me, it's . . . well, it's rather like what Ryan's uncle suffers from!' she finished in a rush, and even managed to smile at the look of bewilderment that crossed his face as she swung round.

'I should explain,' she said quickly, and did as best she could.

He laughed silently. 'He sounds like a very sensible man, Ryan's uncle,' he said finally. 'But there's one thing that puzzles me, Glamorgan. Where do you fit into all this?'

'What do you mean?' She moved restlessly as she heard footsteps in the lounge.

'Well, we've discussed me, you've made some rather drastic assumptions about me and Sheila, but you yourself are still a totally unknown quantity. A dark horse, Morgan.' His eyes probed her face until she dropped her own.

'So long as I'm not an unknown quantity to myself,' she said a little raggedly, 'that's all that matters, surely?'

'I see,' he said coolly after a moment. 'It's still the brick wall. Very well, Morgan, so be it.' He stood aside and ushered her out of the room. 'For the time being at least,' he added very quietly as they came out into the lounge.

Sheila was standing in the middle of the room looking suspicious. 'It took you a long time to hang up one dress!' she commented tartly.

'Didn't it,' Steve said smoothly. He turned back to Morgan. 'How about a cup of coffee to help with your labours?'

'Yes, thank you,' she said evenly, but avoided Sheila's eyes as she walked past her and into the study.

To put it mildly, for the first half hour in the study, Morgan found it excessively difficult to concentrate on the book. She heard voices sometimes raised in hilarity, sometimes lowered to assume an intimacy that troubled her more than the hilarity. Added to this she kept returning to something Steve had said—you've made some rather drastic assumptions about me and Sheila.

What the hell does that mean? she mused as she stared vacantly out on to the deck. But none of her painful musings could come up with a suitable answer. So she tried valiantly to concentrate on the manuscript before her—only to find that raised other disquieting thoughts.

What other plans could he have for Leonie? And why did she feel so interested in Leonie particularly?

Because of the four women in his book, Leonie appealed to her the most, she realised suddenly as she wielded her pen and automatically deleted the second 's' from 'occasionally' which Steve invariably inserted.

'Doesn't he know it has two "c's" and only one "s"?' she muttered to herself. 'He does it every time without fail!'

She sat with her pen poised, her eyes skimming the lines, and gradually found everything else fading from her mind. She took ten minutes off for lunch and had it from a tray on the desk. Then she plunged straight back to work until several hours later, when she sat back with a sigh and rubbed her aching back.

It was done. The first hundred pages of the novel were now in reasonable order and she had made a note of those pages that needed retyping. She glanced at her watch and was surprised to see it was four-thirty. It also dawned on her then that she hadn't heard much movement in the house for a while.

Perhaps they were resting, she thought, and chewed the end of her pen. If she started typing she might disturb them. She stood up and looked around irresolutely, and nearly jumped out of her skin when the door clicked open behind her.

Steve stood there with two tall glasses in his hands.

'I heard the chair,' he said, 'and thought it was time you stopped anyway. You've been at it for hours. Shall we have our drinks on the deck?' He motioned towards the louvred doors.

'Thank you,' she said slowly. 'I've finished, at least the minor corrections, and I've sorted the copies and put each set into a file. There are a few pages that will need retyping, though.'

'You've done well,' he complimented her as he glanced

briefly at the tidy desk.

Morgan followed him out on to the deck and breathed deeply of the clear cool air. Birds were twittering in the gum trees at the end of their long day and the view sped away like a magic carpet before them.

She sank into a canvas chair and sipped her drink. Steve was lounging against the wooden railing. 'It's so peaceful,' she said as the silence stretched. 'All set for the party? Or is Sheila still slaving away in the kitchen?'

He lifted his eyebrows. 'Sheila went hours ago.'

Morgan stared and then grimaced. 'I didn't hear a thing. Isn't she . . . I mean. . . .'

'Oh, she'll be back. She went home to have her beauty sleep and get herself all togged up. She doesn't live far away—down there, in fact.' He pointed down towards the beautiful Samford Valley.

'Oh,' said Morgan, at a momentary loss. Then, 'Well, if there's anything I can do . . .?'

'Not a thing,' he said promptly. 'It's all done, and besides, you've done enough for one day. You deserve time to relax.'

She narrowed her eyes thoughtfully. 'What time does the party start?' she asked a moment later.

'Seven, thereabouts. Does that bother you?' he asked lightly.

'Well, no,' she said a little uncertainly. 'That is . . . no.'

Oh, but it sure does, she told herself, more truthfully. Two and a half hours!

Steve said with a slight shrug, 'I'd like to show you my garden before the light fades and what I've done on my thesis this week, too. Think that might stretch it out?' he queried acutely.

Morgan coloured and tried to say something, but whatever it was, it was so hopelessly disjointed she had to break off and return his teasing grin rather ruefully.

He straightened up and held out his hand. 'Come,' he

invited gently. 'Bring your drink. I haven't introduced you to Sylvester yet, have I?'

She went with him, grateful but at the same time with a lump in her throat because this gentler side of Steve Harrow reminded her so vividly of her hero-worshipping days and all their attendant miseries.

But for heaven's sake don't start feeling sorry for yourself, Morgan, she told herself tartly. But then again, Morgan replied to Morgan, I can't help wondering if this inoculation business isn't going to be a recipe for disaster.

Their tour of Steve's vegetable garden and chicken house was accomplished in complete amiability. Truth to tell, Morgan found she was fascinated, especially with his chickens.

'My mother used to keep chickens,' she said. 'It used to be my job to collect the eggs. Are they laying any better? We used to feed them ... let's see,' she went on with a faraway look in her eyes, 'that was it, cracked corn and some shell grit. My mother always swore by corn as a high energy food and ... I'm not sure about the shell grit. Do you think it makes the eggshells harder?' she asked laughingly. 'Oh,' she added as her eyes fell on Sylvester the rooster, 'isn't he pretty!'

'Maybe that's his problem,' her companion said wryly. 'Perhaps the ladies think he's unfair competition. I should have got a tough old scraggy rooster.'

Morgan was still smiling at this as she went through his latest work on his thesis. 'You might end up as famous as Doctor Leakey or Margaret Mead,' she said enthusiastically. 'You have a way of making it marvellously entertaining. Are you ... have you done all the field work?'

'Some. Why? Do you have a yen to be trekking to Central Australia?' he asked with one raised eyebrow. 'I could use an assistant.'

'Oh no,' she said hurriedly, and moved out of the pool of lamplight they were both standing in beside his desk. 'I mean,' she went on confusedly, 'not that I wouldn't like to see it. . . .'

'But not with me,' he supplied, his blue eyes amused and mocking as he looked her up and down.

She hesitated and thought fleetingly that for some reason the truce they had enjoyed for the last couple of hours seemed to be at an end. And he had ended it himself just then, very deliberately.

She said with a calm she was far from feeling, 'Not particularly. I'm sure we'd get on each other's nerves pretty soon.' She grinned. 'My nasty tongue would get the better of me, I'm sure!'

'It hasn't been much in evidence today,' he observed. 'I wonder why?'

'I'm trying to turn over a new leaf,' she said with mock gravity in a desperate bid to defuse this encounter. Why do I feel so panicky?, she thought. As if this whole day has been leading up to . . . to some kind of confrontation?

She went on lightly, 'But one day is probably my limit. I'm sure you'd hate to have a virago on your hands while you're trying to work.' She turned away. 'I think I ought to start getting ready now.'

'Sure,' Steve said offhandedly a moment later. 'It's all yours—the bedroom and bathroom, I mean. Don't forget to lock yourself in,' he added softly but with a flashing look of blue fire as she moved past him.

She tightened her lips and tossed her head involuntarily, but forbore to reply.

'And I'll do just that,' she muttered to herself as she entered the bedroom. She closed the door behind her and leant back against it, finding her legs curiously shaky. She took a deep breath and straightened up, then turned back to the door, but with her fingers on the key, she hesitated.

Then she shrugged and moved away with the door still unlocked. He wouldn't do it, she told herself. For two reasons, he's probably so sure I will lock it, he could be out there laughing at me right now.

She ground her teeth. Well, come on, what's the other reason, Morgan? she asked herself tautly.

But she discovered the second reason was hers. If he does have any intentions I can show him for once and for all that I'm immune to him. Particularly on the day after the night before, she thought confusedly. Let him concentrate on Miss Sheila Somerville!

But she did lock the bathroom door.

CHAPTER SIX

'My dear, you have the most wonderful *skin*. It has a quality of iridescence that's incredible! And as for that garment you're wearing, I'm sure it comes straight from Paris!'

Morgan coughed and observed her elderly admirer speculatively over the rim of her glass. The party was in full swing—for the most part a collection of well-groomed, interesting people whom she had enjoyed meeting. Even this man with his shock of white hair and goatee beard interested her because his eyes sparkled with intelligence and wit, despite his preoccupation with her skin.

'Has anyone ever painted you?' he went on, unperturbed by her silence. 'You know, I can picture you alongside the Botticelli Venus.'

Morgan swallowed and spluttered on a mouthful of brandy and ginger ale.

'Or,' he added meditatively, 'you know, under certain lights your hair would have interested Titian, I'm sure.'

She cleared her throat. 'Do you paint?' she asked ingenuously.

'I do. I don't know if I could do justice to you, though, my dear,' he said gravely. 'Hey, Steve,' he turned to call over his shoulder. 'Come and introduce me to this pearl among pearls. How long have you been hiding her light under a bushel, by the way, old buddy?'

Morgan blushed vividly as she became the cynosure of all eyes and then shivered as she encountered an icy glance from Sheila, who was a vision of fair, Nordic loveliness in pale ice-blue.

Steve came to her rescue. 'Now don't embarrass her,

Mike,' he said laughingly as he moved towards Morgan and took her elbow in his hand. 'And don't,' he added so that only the three of them could hear, 'insult her. She's liable to knock you out.'

'I am not!' Morgan protested.

'Aren't you, sweetheart?' he murmured, and let his eyes play over her bare shoulders that rose smooth and white from her black dress that gleamed as she moved and the light caught the oblong metallic sequins that encrusted the material.

It was the essence of simplicity, her dress, a tight-fitting sheath that clung to her as if moulded to her figure and held up by narrow straps that crossed over the tops of her breasts and tied at the back of her neck. It was an original creation, but not from Paris. In fact it was the work of an as yet unknown Surfer's Paradise designer, and Morgan wished fervently that she could convey her elderly admirer's remark to its creator.

Nevertheless, beneath Steve Harrow's probing gaze now and the curious glint in his eyes she had detected when she had emerged earlier from his bedroom, having achieved her toilette without any interruptions, she couldn't help wishing she hadn't worn the dress.

I fell victim to a purely feminine whim, she thought, a desire to outshine every other girl in the room. What a strange time to want to flex my femininity, she thought wryly. But a glimpse of Sheila across the room talking animatedly to a good-looking man as she unconsciously preened her hair and smoothed her ice-blue dress across her hips brought a kind of philosophical acceptance to Morgan. I'm not the only one, anyway. . . .

She also felt a lessening of her hostility towards the other girl, she found, and had to admit to herself that this had been growing since the morning. If she's going through one quarter of the trauma I am, who wouldn't feel sorry for her,' she mused.

These FOUR free Harlequin Presents novels allow you to enter the world of romance, love and desire. As a member of the Harlequin Home Subscription Plan, you can continue to experience all the moods of love. You'll be inspired by moments so real...so moving...you won't want them to end. So start your own Harlequin Presents adventure by returning the reply card below. <u>DO IT TODAY!</u>

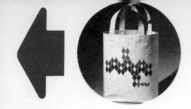

EXTRA BONUS
MAIL YOUR ORDER
TODAY AND GET A
FREE TOTE BAG
FROM HARLEQUIN.

Later in the evening, after the delicious buffet had been consumed and cleared away, someone dimmed the lights and moved the furniture around, then set the record player to some energetic disco music.

Morgan danced animatedly, never short of a partner and amazed to find herself feeling quite at home among Steve's friends, although she didn't miss the odd speculative glance that came her way. It was a mixed bag of guests, she found academics, artists of one sort of another, one man who told her happily that he bred earthworms on a commercial basis, several intense, formidably intelligent women and several matronly, motherly ones. But all seemingly warm, genuinely friendly people.

Well, almost all, she amended, as she danced animatedly with the earthworm producer and marvelled secretly at how she'd managed to lose so many inhibitions in the space of one evening. Not only had she never danced this way before, she thought dazedly, but she'd even managed to parry an invitation to view her partner's worms—an invitation delivered in a manner that left her in no doubt that it was a variation of the old 'come up and see my etchings' routine—with a smile and a phrase that made him stop dancing and laugh uproariously.

I'm putting on a show, she thought as they started to dance again. A show for the gallery. Or . . . or for him? Steve?

Yes, for him, she acknowledged later when people were starting to make their farewells, and in a rare quiet moment she stood on the deck and let the cool breeze play on her overheated skin. To show him he needn't feel sorry for me or guilty or. . . .

She stiffened slightly at a step behind her and knew it was him through some sixth sense. Knew it, but didn't resist as his arms slid around her waist from behind.

She even let herself lean back against him, but she said

huskily, 'No. I knew it was all leading up to this, but the answer is no.'

He didn't reply and some treacherous person changed the record so that music was slow and dreamy. Then he spoke. 'Won't you even dance with me, Morgan? You've danced with everyone else tonight.'

'I . . . I think I should go,' she said unevenly. 'It's getting late.'

She trembled as she felt his mouth on her hair.

'You can't,' he murmured indistinctly, and his hands came up to cup her breasts from beneath.

'Why . . . why can't I?' she whispered, and realised her breath was coming in gasps as she tried to ignore his lips and fingers and the sensations they were arousing in her.

'Why can't you?' he said after a long moment. 'Because you were first in, you're effectively hemmed in—your car, I mean—until everyone else is gone. That's why,' he murmured, and bent his head to kiss her neck.

Morgan made a determined effort and turned within the circle of his arms. 'Don't,' she pleaded raggedly. 'What will everyone think?'

'What a lucky devil I am,' he said quietly, unsmilingly, his eyes resting intently on her lips. 'The men will, anyway.'

'And the . . . women?' she whispered painfully. She looked over his shoulder as she spoke, to see Sheila standing in the middle of the room, suddenly illuminated as someone switched on the overhead light and with a pathetically white, tight face as she gazed out towards them.

Morgan sucked in a breath and closed her eyes. Then she tried to free herself, but found that while Steve had let his arms drop and moved back a pace, he caught her wrist in a grip of steel. 'Not *just* yet . . . Morgan,' he said, his lips barely moving but his eyes glittering in a way that frightened her.

She started to pull away, but changed her mind almost

immediately as she realised she wouldn't escape without an undignified struggle.

'That's better,' he said quietly, and turned back to the lounge-room. He slid his fingers through hers and drew her inside with him, making it look as if they were holding hands casually as they said goodbye to the rest of his guests.

And when it was Sheila's turn finally to say goodbye, Morgan tensed painfully, expecting she knew not what, but Sheila surprised her. For the aggression she had exhibited earlier was gone and in its place there was only a blank, mute acceptance.

Acceptance? Of what? Morgan wondered dazedly. Of the fact that I've supplanted her? Oh, no, I hate this!

She moved her fingers convulsively, but Steve's grip on them only tightened. Yet he was curiously gentle with Sheila, she couldn't help noticing amid her own turbulent emotions, and as Sheila left with a laughing group of people the only indication he gave that he had noticed the sheen of tears in her pale eyes was a sudden restless movement of his shoulders.

And finally they were alone as the sound of the last car engine faded into the night.

Morgan pulled her hand away and stood irresolute in the middle of the room, half turned away from him, her head bent, her heart beating suffocatingly.

She heard him moving quietly around the room. The central light went out and one other lamp, leaving the room dim and shadowy with the feathery pampas grass heads reflected hugely on one wall. The record player came to life again and the room was filled with soft sensuous music.

And yet I've never felt more frightened in my life, Morgan thought. I want to run, but I can't move. I want to go, but I want to stay. I want to stay despite the fact that there's no satisfactory way he can explain how he could sleep with Sheila last night and . . . and me tonight. I don't want to bother with anything like that.

She lifted her head wearily at last to see him lounging against a doorway, his hands thrust into his pockets and with his tie off and his shirt unbuttoned at the neck. Their eyes clashed across the intervening space and there was an air of unbelievable tension in the room.

She shivered slightly and dropped her eyes. 'I . . . I . . .' she began haltingly. 'I really should go,' she finished lamely.

'Should you?' said Steve expressionlessly. 'Why don't you, then? I won't stop you.'

She turned away slowly and was mortified to feel tears on her cheeks. She dashed at them angrily and stumbled blindly across the room towards the bedroom to retrieve her suitcase and her purse.

He was there at the same doorway as she came out of the bedroom, and she stopped uncertainly as he straightened up and came towards her.

He stopped in front of her and reached out a hand to lift up the warm jacket she had slung across her arm. 'It's cold out there, Morgan. Better put it on.' He slipped it around her shoulders and then stepped back to say impersonally, 'Drive carefully, won't you? You're only running away from yourself, you know. So take it easy on the slopes.'

'I . . . I'm not,' she stammered. 'You're just trying to make me feel as if I am.'

'Why the tears, then?' he drawled ironically. 'Are they for me?'

'No . . . yes . . . no! I don't know,' she said unsteadily.

'No, I don't think you do,' he said on a curiously rough note. 'But you're not stupid—I know that. So there can be only one reason why you can walk away from me in this state, Glamorgan. You're a coward.'

'I'm not,' she flung at him, her shoulders suddenly squared.

'But you are,' he said on a steely note. 'You want me as

much as I want you. Yes, I do,' he added with a suddenly
wry look as she flinched perceptibly. 'I thought I couldn't
have made it plainer.'

She set her teeth as he moved forward and took her by
the shoulders. 'Shall I spell it out, Morgan, so there can
be no more misunderstandings?' he asked with an edge of
cold mockery, and tightened his grasp cruelly as she tried
to wrench herself free. 'I want you as I've never wanted
any woman before,' he said deliberately. 'I want to take
you to bed now. I want to slide your clothes off slowly so
that I can savour every inch of your beautiful body, see
you as no man has ever seen you before, touch you and
make you cry out with the unbearable pleasure of it. And
I want to make love to you over and over again until
you're too exhausted to move. And then,' he said, his
voice low and husky and his lids half lowered over his blue,
blue eyes, 'I would gather you into my arms and soothe
you to sleep so gently . . . you're blushing, Morgan.'

'Of course I am,' she whispered, and lifted her hands to
her hot cheeks. 'I . . . I. . . .' She looked around wildly. 'I
can't!' she said jerkily. 'I just can't!'

'Why not?' he asked sombrely, and dropped his hands.

'Because . . . because . . . oh! Didn't you see how she
looked at you?' she cried.

A nerve throbbed in his jaw and he narrowed his eyes.
'Are you trying to hide behind Sheila, Morgan?' he
demanded. 'She has nothing to do with us,' he said tautly.
'She. . . .'

But Morgan put her hands over her ears. 'I don't want
to hear it,' she sobbed. 'If you can explain her away to
me . . . that's what I hate about men,' she cried passion-
ately. 'It's so simple for you, isn't it? Off with the old and
on with the new with a flick of the fingers!'

'Morgan,' he said grimly, and took her wrists in his
hands to wrest them away from her head. '*Listen* to me,
will you!'

But with tears pouring down her cheeks she exerted all her strength to pull away from him, then ran across the room and down the staircase. But in her headlong flight, she missed her footing and her mouth opened in a soundless scream as she felt herself clutching for the railing to break her fall, but finding nothing. Only a void. And then nothing.

Morgan opened her eyes and was amazed to see she was in her own bedroom, although she had no recollection of how she got there. She licked her lips which felt dry and cracked and winced as the movement caused a searing pain to shoot through her head.

She waited a few minutes before making any more incautious moves, and then slowly turned her head and jumped as she encountered, of all people, Brad Smith, looking unusually clean and tidy. And anxious.

'What are you doing here?' she asked feebly as he straightened from his lounging position astride her dressing table stool.

He didn't answer immediately but sidled to the door and called through it, 'She's awake, Mum!'

He crossed back to the bed and stood there looking down at her gingerly. 'How you you feel, Morgan? Boy, you've got the best shiner I've ever seen!' His tone was almost reverent.

Morgan's hand flew to one eye as she digested this news incredulously. 'I . . . I. . . .' she stammered.

'He reckons,' Brad went on with a jerk of his head, 'that you fell down the stairs. Looks to me like he went to plant one on you, though. . . .'

'Brad!' His mother's sharp tones cut across his sentence. 'Whatever are you saying to Morgan? Off you go now.' Molly Smith bustled across the room and forcibly ejected the light of her life, who also happened to be a great trial to her and almost everyone else he came in contact with.

'That boy!' she said severely as she plunged back across the room to straighten Morgan's sheets. 'He'll be the death of me! How do you feel, love?' she went on in more soothing tones.

'I ... I'm not quite sure,' Morgan said hesitantly. 'What ... how ... have I really got a black eye?'

'Mmm,' Molly said regretfully. 'Also a nasty bump on your head. But you're not to worry, love,' she added. 'In a few days you'll be as right as rain. He ... Mr Harrow, that is, did all the right things. He took you to hospital and they X-rayed your skull for fractures, but there's nothing like that, just a bit of concussion. They kept you in a couple of nights and now you're back home he's arranged for a doctor to come and see you every day for the next few days. Don't you remember any of it, Morgan?'

Morgan bit her lip ruefully. 'Yes, I do,' she said slowly. 'It's all coming back. I even remember coming home from the hospital this morning ... was it this morning?'

'Yes. They said you'd feel a bit groggy for a little while.' Molly straightened up. 'Now, how about a little morsel of lunch? I've steamed a nice young chook .... do you think you could eat some?'

'Yes. Thank you,' Morgan said dazedly. 'Are you ... but you must have so much to do at home,' she added anxiously.

'Not for today I haven't,' Molly declared stoutly, 'so don't you worry your head about it. And for the nights he ... that is, Mr Harrow, is going to take care of them. He's a very capable man, isn't he? I'll be back in a tick, love!'

And she left the room, unaware or at least uncommenting of the fact that Morgan's mouth was hanging open slackly as she digested this bit of information.

She slept on and off after partaking of Molly Smith's 'nice young chook', although she felt she should be concentrating on the problem of Steve Harrow, but she just didn't seem to have the energy to do more than doze fitfully.

It was Ryan who roused her as the sun set. He peeped round the door and then advanced towards the bed brandishing a huge bunch of roses, a new paperback and a box of chocolates.

'Morgan,' he said laughingly as her eyes flickered open.

'Don't!' she said weakly but with an answering grin on her face as she pulled herself up on the pillows.

'Have you seen yourself?' he asked, still grinning hugely.

'No,' she said crossly, then she relented. 'I'm not game to look. But I have it on the best authority that it's a . . . good one.'

'Honey, it's a beauty,' said Ryan. He pulled up a chair and laid his offerings on the bed. 'Now just tell me,' he added with mock sternness, 'what you've been doing to yourself, young lady. I can't let you out of my sight for a minute!'

'I . . . fell down some stairs,' she said, and shivered as for the first time she relived the awful sensation of falling through space. 'How did you know?'

'Steve,' he said laconically. 'He rang us first thing Monday morning—yesterday—and told us not to expect you back for at least two weeks. I'm the official bearer of everyone's sympathy, by the way. Including the boss, who specifically made a point of saying you're not to worry about work, we'll cope until you're quite sure you're better.'

'Thank you,' Morgan murmured emotionally as she opened the card attached to the roses to find that it was signed by everyone at work. 'You're all very sweet.'

She blinked away a tear or two and noticed that his expression was suddenly sober. Here it comes, she thought.

'Did you fall down some stairs, Morgan?' he asked quietly. 'Or is there something you'd like to tell me . . . friend?' He stressed the last word.

'I . . . did,' she said haltingly. 'It's true. But it was because I was . . . upset. It was all my own silly fault really.'

'Did he upset you, Morgan?' he asked intently.

She didn't answer but plucked at the sheet agitatedly.

'It must have been him, I reckon,' Ryan said slowly. 'Why else would he be the one on hand, the one to take you to hospital? The one to make all these arrangements? Morgan, if you want, I'd be willing to try and make sure he stays away from you for ever,' he said urgently.

'I . . . I. . . .' She shrugged and smiled faintly. 'I haven't seen him since it happened. I don't remember the hospital—I mean, how I got there, but he wasn't there when I woke up. And he wasn't there when they brought me home in an ambulance today. But he must have arranged everything with Mrs Smith, and you say he rang . . . work?'

Ryan sat back and narrowed his eyes thoughtfully. 'I see,' he said at last.

Morgan shot him a startled glance. 'What do you see?' she asked with a puzzled frown.

'Oh, nothing,' he said casually. 'Er . . . according to your Mrs Smith, there's a registered nurse coming to stay with you tonight—by the way——' He stopped abruptly. 'What's the matter? Didn't you know?'

'No. No, I didn't,' she said confusedly. 'I thought . . . actually I hadn't thought about it,' she added hurriedly, and smiled across at him. 'What were you going to say? By the way what?'

Ryan raised his eyebrows quizzically and didn't answer for a minute. Then he said, 'Oh yes. There's a mob of terrible-looking kids hanging round your front door. Do they give you any trouble?'

Morgan laughed softly, then coloured as she visualised Brad passing on his version of her injury to the rest of the street. 'Not really,' she said with a little sigh. 'Actually I'm quite fond of . . . most of them.'

They talked desultorily for a while longer, and then the arrival of the nurse together with Molly Smith's fond departure caused Ryan to say he should be getting home too. He took his leave in his own inimitable manner, kissing Morgan fondly and admonishing her to take care. But she didn't miss the curious spark of speculation that still lingered in his eyes.

I wish I didn't have the feeling that he's up to something devious, she thought to herself as she submitted to the night nurse's ministrations a little uncomfortably. But the woman was a cheerful happy person and before long she was chatting away to Morgan as she moved round the bedroom tidying it up so that Morgan felt less strange, less confused and finally marvelling at how a total stranger could have put her at her ease like this.

'You're very kind, Mrs Spencer,' she murmured sleepily, feeling like a small child, cosseted and pampered. It was a long time since she'd felt like this, she realised, just before she drifted off to sleep.

The nurse pulled the covers up gently and observed Morgan's bruised sleeping face with a sudden lessening of her cheerful smile.

'So young,' she muttered with a shake of her grey curls. 'And for all you're supposed to have fallen down some stairs, I'll bet the truth of it is that you tangled with a *man*, Miss Jones!'

'There!' The doctor put away his little light with which he had been gazing into her pupils, together with his other gear. He had examined her thoroughly. 'Seems to be all shipshape,' he commented.

She grimaced and touched her eye lightly.

'I know.' He smiled sympathetically. 'But you must admit it's improving! And in a day or two it will have faded completely.'

'I hope so,' she sighed. 'Does this mean I can get back to normal now?'

'More or less.' He glanced at her keenly. 'But I would advise you to take things easily for at least another week. And if you suffer from any headaches or any other unusual symptoms, let me know immediately.'

'I . . . don't have to be nursed any longer, do I?' she asked hesitantly.

'No, Miss Jones. Although I wouldn't discourage your very kind neighbours from helping you out. They seem to enjoy it so,' he added with a humorous twinkle in his eye.

She smiled back at him and pleated the bedcover with her fingers. 'I . . . I suppose I owe you some money,' she said. 'I. . . .'

'Not me, my dear,' he interrupted briskly. 'In fact your account is fully up to date. Now you look after yourself, Miss Jones,' he said cheerfully. 'And stay away from tricky staircases, won't you!'

And with a pat on the shoulder he left Morgan staring round-eyed after him.

'Thank you. No . . . no, that's all, thank you,' Morgan said into the phone, and put it down dazedly. As with the doctor, her hospital bills had all been paid, and the home nursing charges too.

'And it isn't Ryan,' she murmured to herself. She knew this because on one of his frequent visits Ryan had very tactfully tried to discover how she was placed financially. She had assured him she had no problems, at the same time as she fought down a feeling of panic. Because, unlike her father, she herself had no qualms about a free public health service—certainly not the one the State of Queensland offered, and with this in mind, had never bothered to take out medical insurance. Never dreaming, she thought bitterly, that I could end up in a very expensive private nursing home so stunned I didn't really know where I was. . . .

Steve Harrow must have paid for it all.

'It must have been him.' She echoed her thoughts out aloud. 'But why haven't I seen him?'

She stared at her reflection in the dressing-table mirror. 'Not once, unless I don't remember it,' she mused. She fingered the purple bruises around her eye. 'It's nearly a week since it happened. He's paid all my bills, he made all the arrangements. Would he do that if he was very angry with me because I . . . because I wouldn't . . . ?'

She dropped her head wearily into her hands. Not even a flower, she thought miserably. Just nothing. Why? she asked herself, and felt the weak silly tears, which seemed to come so easily these days, trickle through her fingers.

She raised her head and licked the salty moisture from her lips. I look a fright, she thought miserably. And worse, I feel a fright! I feel as if Steve's washed his hands of me for once and for all. But this time he's picked up the tab too, literally, so he doesn't have to have me on his conscience.

But isn't that what you wanted, Morgan? she asked herself.

Isn't it?

The answer eluded her, though, she found as she searched her reflection in the glass with tragic eyes.

The next morning the doorbell chimed as she was clearing the remains of her breakfast.

'Come in,' she called, thinking it was bound to be Molly Smith. 'The door's not locked. How are you, Molly?' she added as she heard the door open. 'I'm just washing the dishes.'

She frowned as there was no reply and walked into the lounge with the dishcloth still in her hand—and promptly dropped it as her mouth formed a soundless O of astonishment.

For it was not Molly Smith but Sheila Somerville who stood in the middle of her lounge room clutching a huge bunch of carnations.

'What . . . how . . . I mean. . . .' Morgan stammered.

Sheila came forward slowly. 'Oh, my dear,' she said compassionately, 'you are in a mess!' Her eyes flickered over Morgan who was still in her dressing gown and came back to her face. She frowned. 'I brought you some flowers and a book,' she added absently, and laid both offerings down on the table while she continued to stare at Morgan.

It was a long uncomfortable moment later that she said abruptly, 'Did Steve do that? He *said* you fell down some stairs. . . .'

'I did,' Morgan interrupted swiftly.

Sheila smiled slightly. 'I'm afraid that rather sounds like a variation of the old walking into a door routine, pet! Still, I find it hard to believe of Steve.'

Morgan counted to ten rather swiftly beneath her breath. Then she said lightly, 'Well, don't. Because I can assure you he didn't do it.'

Sheila chuckled suddenly. 'I won't, then,' she promised gaily. 'Is that the gorgeous aroma of fresh coffee I smell?' she asked.

'Er . . . yes,' Morgan replied, trying to gather her scattered wits. 'I was just going to have a cup, would you like to join me?' She glanced at the beautiful carnations and thought, it's the least I can do, I guess.

'Love to,' said Sheila, and sat down with her perfect legs displayed to advantage beneath a fine angora suit that was the same ice-blue as her eyes.

Morgan turned to the kitchen and couldn't help thinking a little viciously that if there was one thing worse than having a black eye, it was to be caught in your dressing gown with it. And as she poured the coffee she couldn't help wondering, also, just what was behind this visit. She realised too that despite her feelings of compassion for Sheila, remembered from the night of the party, she was now feeling just a little wary of the other girl.

But she didn't allow any of this to show as she served the coffee and sat down herself with all the savoir-faire she could muster and all that was possible clad in a rather threadbare but much-beloved pink candlewick dressing gown that had belonged to her mother.

She eyed Sheila over the rim of her cup and said the first thing that came into her head. 'How's Steve? I haven't. . . .' Her voice faltered and she could have bitten her tongue. 'I haven't seen him lately,' she finished a little lamely.

Sheila was silent for a long moment and then she said abruptly, 'Morgan, I have to be honest with you. That's the main reason I came to see you—about Steve. To give you some advice, as a matter of fact.'

'Oh yes?' Morgan said faintly, and swallowed.

'You see, I've known him a long time,' Sheila said seriously, and crossed her legs gracefully.

'So have I,' Morgan replied, and wondered what had prompted her to say it. Maybe it was the proprietorial tone in Sheila's voice.

'Well then,' Sheila said equably, 'perhaps you don't need me to tell you that he won't ever marry you?'

Morgan raised her eyebrows ironically. 'No, I don't. But I'd like to know why you felt you should try.'

'Well, I felt a bit sorry for you when I heard what had happened—more so now that I've seen you, pet!' Sheila added with a grin. Then she sobered and sat forward earnestly. 'Look, Morgan, put it this way, Steve's girlfriends come and go. What would be the fun of joining a long list of discards? Do you see what I mean?'

Oh, I do, Morgan thought acidly. After all, I've told myself virtually the same thing often enough. Why then should it be so peculiarly annoying to have Sheila tell me it?

She pursed her lips thoughtfully and pondered. I've bared my soul to Ryan, she thought; maybe I should bare it to Sheila. But a demon of perversity claimed her as she eyed the other girl. Is it my imagination, or does she look incredibly smug? she wondered as Sheila ostentatiously examined her perfectly manicured fingernails.

Yes, she does! Morgan decided as Sheila looked up and their eyes met. Well, here goes.

'Sheila,' she said quietly, 'I appreciate your coming here and your gifts and your advice. But I have to tell you that you're approaching your problem from the wrong angle.'

An expression of wary alertness crossed the other girl's face. 'What do you mean?' she asked coldly.

'This. Manipulating me out of the way is unnecessary and pointless, Sheila. I don't constitute any threat to you. In fact I've worked very hard and I think successfully at removing *myself* from the scene.' She stopped abruptly as a shaft of pain seemed to pierce her heart. She swallowed and then forced herself to go on. 'If you're the woman he wants finally, you'll be one very lucky girl. If you're not the one he wants, all the scheming in the world won't alter it, and I doubt very much whether you'll rise at all in his estimation if you consistently set out to remove all the opposition. It's a waiting game you have to play, dear, and I really feel sorry for you. . . .'

'Stop it!' Sheila hissed as she jumped to her feet, her beautiful features contorted with anger. 'How dare you! You know nothing of what's passed between us. You . . . you patronising bitch!'

Morgan sat back wearily. 'No, I don't,' she conceded. 'But I'm not blind. If I've misread it all and mistrusted your motives, I'm sorry. Very sorry.' She winced at the naked emotion in the other girl's eyes which told just as effectively as any words that she had misread nothing. How could I have been so cruel? she thought.

She stood up herself. 'Sheila. . . .' she tried to put her hand on the other girl's arm, but Sheila shook it off.

'Take your hands off me!' Sheila spat at her, and with a mindless fury strode across to the table where the carnations lay and ripped the wrapping from them and hurled them across the room. Then she picked up the book and deliberately tore out the last few pages and kept tearing at them until the pieces were little larger than confetti.

'There!' she said with her throat working convulsively and tears streaming down her cheeks. 'I just hope I never lay eyes on you again, Morgan Jones, because I couldn't guarantee I wouldn't scratch your eyes out and ruin that beautiful skin too!'

And she flung out of the flat, slamming the door, leaving Morgan staring after her with wide, incredulous eyes and parted lips.

CHAPTER SEVEN

THE Monday of her second week of convalescence dawned calm and cold. Morgan contemplated another week of inactivity and found herself feeling strangely restless.

The nasty little scene with Sheila had refused to be put out of mind and seemed to be even more prominent if anything on this Monday with school claiming most of her youthful friends and even Brad Smith—against his better judgment.

In fact her flat was an oasis of sparkling clean peace and quiet and about as inviting as an endless vista of lunar landscape.

Her black eye had finally faded to no more than a subtle shading beneath her lower lid as if she'd had too many sleepless nights, but her reflection in the mirror didn't afford her any more pleasure without it than it had with it.

I don't look . . . glossy any more, she thought as she stared at herself. It was mid-morning and she'd done every conceivable chore she could find to do. She reached for her make-up kit and deftly applied a cover-up operation.

'That's worse,' she said gloomily to her reflection. 'Now I look old.'

She cleansed her face of every scrap of make-up and pulled her hair back into an uncompromising bun. Then she turned to her wardrobe and drew from it a warm comfortable tracksuit. And once dressed, without giving herself time to think, she snatched up her car keys.

Waterworks Road was relatively deserted at this time of day and she was through the Gap in a surprisingly

short time. And it was as suburbia fell away that she began
to panic.

'After all you said to Sheila, Morgan,' she chided herself, 'how could you have the nerve . . .?'

'But this has nothing to do with Sheila,' she replied to
herself, and then amended her reply. 'At least, nothing to
do with Sheila and Steve. This is purely business. I simply
can't accept his charity, that's all!'

'You could have written,' an unkind inner voice
prompted.

'Yes, I could have,' she acknowledged wearily. 'But I
didn't. And while I'm on the subject, yes, I suspect I
couldn't bear the thought of never seeing him again, and
I wasn't quite honest with Sheila either. But if I'd told
her how I really feel about Steve. . . .'

And for the hundredth time Sheila's face, contorted and
ugly, flashed into her mind's eye. That was what it could
do to one if you let it get to you, she thought as she
changed gear to cope with the steeper grades of Mount
Nebo. Dear God!

There was no car parked beneath the deck, she noted
with a distinct feeling of who cares anyway, as she nosed
the Mini into the space.

'All right, Morgan,' she muttered to herself, 'if you're
not sure why you're here, you'd better start thinking
quickly, mate!'

She stepped out of the car and wandered into the sunshine. The house was quiet above her. Somehow or
another it had a deserted air, she thought. And yet as she
turned round she noticed that the front door stood ajar.

She shrugged and was about to knock, when the sound
of an axe chopping rhythmically came to her ears.

She hesitated and dropped her hand. The sound seemed
to be coming from behind the house. She picked her way
up the rough incline between the tall gums, sniffing the
clear morning air that was warm in the belated sunlight,

and felt a trickle of perspiration run down her back between her shoulder blades.

It was Steve Harrow chopping wood with precise, powerful strokes that split the logs cleanly and caused the axe-head to reflect the dappled sunlight with each arc. He had his back to her and she guessed he hadn't heard her approach. She sank down on to a tree-stump and found that her heart had leapt uncomfortably into her mouth at the sight of him. He had his shirt off and she watched the muscles of his back and shoulders ripple with each stroke, with a kind of fearful fascination.

His sudden change of movement took her by surprise as he laid the axe down and said, still with his back to her, 'How are you, Morgan?' He bent to stack the logs in a pile at his feet.

Her colour fluctuated. 'I'm fine,' she said huskily. 'How did you know I was here?'

'I heard the car earlier,' he said. 'Your engine has a particular pinging sound.' He turned round unexpectedly and she scrambled up hastily.

Their eyes met briefly and then he turned back to the logs. 'You look a lot better,' he said casually, and transferred some logs into a wheelbarrow.

She bit her lip and thought confusedly, this is going to be even harder than I anticipated. She said tentatively, 'I . . . I came to thank you. Also to. . . .' She trailed off uncertainly.

He straightened up and turned round fully with the loaded wheelbarrow. 'To what?' he queried.

'To pay you back,' she finished in a rush. 'You see, I can claim it on . . . on my medical benefit.'

One eyebrow rose and she could have bitten her tongue at her hesitation.

'All of it?' he asked.

'Most of it,' she said quite untruthfully.

'Really?' he said on a satirical note that brought her

eyes, which had been riveted to her shoes, flying to his face. He added as he reached for his shirt, 'If you think you could share a cup of coffee with me without succumbing to an urge to throw yourself over the deck, I think we should go in and discuss this.'

Morgan opened her mouth to protest, but he took not the slightest notice and pushed the wheelbarrow past her so that she was forced to follow him down the track to the house. At the back door she started to speak again, but somehow her words died on her lips at his set expression as he methodically packed the wood into a basket and then swung it on to his shoulder and pushed the back door open with his foot.

She took a deep breath and followed him inside, feeling rather like a dog at his heels.

'Sit down, Morgan,' he said over his shoulder as he placed the basket beside the fireplace.

She hovered and found herself saying, 'I'll make the coffee if you like.'

'O.K. I'll have a quick shower in the meantime.' He walked out of the lounge without a backward glance.

Morgan stared after him with stricken eyes. He's totally disgusted with me, she thought, and was amazed at the pain she felt. She gathered herself slowly as she heard the shower gush and with stumbling footsteps moved into the kitchen.

They sat on the deck sipping their coffee in the sunlight and Morgan felt about as uncomfortable as it was possible to be, she thought. Each conversational gambit that came into her head seemed to be the essence of trivia and she abandoned it unspoken and finally gave her mind to the sheer magic of the view and the aromatic coffee that steamed gently in her cup.

Let him make the first move, she thought rebelliously, because the mere fact of him sitting opposite her was enough to make her tongue-tied.

She flicked him a quick glance, to see he was looking out over the deck. He looked quite at ease too, with his hair still damp from the shower and clad in fresh but faded jeans and a khaki bush shirt that had seen better days.

So much for your visions of sartorial elegance, Morgan, she thought. He doesn't give two hoots for what he wears. Is it a form of arrogance or is it just a sort of confidence he has that doesn't need any false bolstering up?

She raised her eyes again and flushed to see that he was looking at her thoughtfully now, but enigmatically.

He said, 'Your eye. It's almost back to normal.'

Her hand flew up to touch it involuntarily. 'It was a real shiner,' she said gruffly. 'Brad . . . I mean one of the kids I—attempt to tutor, was almost impressed.'

'Brad Smith, you mean?'

'Yes,' she said ruefully. 'I don't suppose you know him, but beneath all his bravado, he's not a bad kid.'

'I do know him,' Steve returned with a slight grin. 'And I feel for his mother. I gather he suffers from the lack of a father who absented himself a few years back?'

'Yes, he does,' she said, her interest caught. 'He . . . well, he needs a strong man.' She grimaced. 'It's a bit sad really to see that potential go wasting.'

He swirled the liquid in his cup and said absently, 'I hope you're right. I'm taking him on a field trip with me next vacation.'

'Brad Smith?' she said incredulously. 'Are you joking?'

'Why should I be?' he countered. 'You tutor him, don't you?'

'Well, yes, but . . . I mean, how did this come about?'

He shrugged. 'His mother, bless her inquisitive soul, came to investigate when she saw me going into your flat that Sunday. I was getting some gear for you. After I'd explained myself and why I was not only entering your flat but also driving your car, she became most helpful

and offered to keep an eye on you when you came home.'
He broke off with a wry twist of his lips. 'Offered isn't
quite the right word—demanded, more like it. Anyway,
the day you were due to come out, I went to see her to
tell her what time to expect you home and I inadvertently
arrived just as the police were leaving.'

'The police?' Morgan echoed, wide-eyed. 'You mean
on account of Brad?'

'Uh-huh.' He stared broodingly down at his coffee.
'He'd been caught shoplifting and wagging school.'

Morgan sighed exasperatedly. 'Are they going to charge
him?'

'No. As a matter of fact I was most impressed by their
methods. They took into account that it was more in the
nature of a feat of bravado, I suppose you could say, and
they gave him a severe warning.'

'No wonder he looked so ... deflated,' Morgan said
slowly. 'In fact he still does. But why didn't anyone tell
me this?' she demanded.

'I suppose they didn't want to worry you,' he said.

'So you offered to try and sort him out,' she said after a
moment.

Steve grimaced. 'I couldn't help feeling sorry for both
of them. I think his mother is quietly desperate. But I
thought to ... perhaps broaden his mind and offer him
some masculine company rather than sort him out.'

'You're very kind,' Morgan commented, and thought,
another lame duck! He must have a penchant for it. She
squirmed uncomfortably in her chair at the thought of
sharing that category with, of all people, Brad Smith!

But it's probably true, she told herself. I must be in the
lame duck class now. I mean, for a man who told me he
wanted me more than he'd ever 'wanted'—why do I find
that word so suspect?—anyone, he's remarkably cool if
not downright icy. Where are you, Sheila Somerville?

She looked at him from beneath her lashes as he set his

coffee cup down and stretched luxuriously, lacing his fingers behind his head. If only I could get into his mind, she thought wonderingly. I have this feeling we're in two different leagues and, worse, that I'll never attain his league. I wonder if Sheila feels the same?

She said, 'I'm sorry about last . . . I mean that Saturday night. I put you to enormous trouble. But I . . . I didn't do it deliberately.'

'Didn't you?' he said expressionlessly, his eyes narrowed against the sun and his gold-tipped lashes casting shadows on his cheek. He sat up. 'I don't suppose you did. Most neurotic people don't think twice before they plunge into their actions.'

Morgan flinched inwardly. 'Is that what you think I am?' she managed to say unsteadily.

'On the evidence, why shouldn't I? All you had to do that night was walk out of here. Unless you thought—despite what I said—that I was going to leap on you and take you by force. Did you think that, Morgan?' He turned to her suddenly, his blue eyes so cold and expressionless that she felt chilled to the marrow.

She took a deep breath. 'No,' she said steadily. 'I . . . no.'

'Well then,' he said softly but with his eyes boring into her own, 'I can think of only one other explanation. You were fleeing from yourself. From the battle raging within *you*. And it was so fierce, you didn't stop to think before tearing down a narrow spiral staircase in high-heeled slippers or whatever you call those flimsy, teetering shoes you were wearing.'

She plaited her fingers nervously and desperately schooled her face to blankness and her voice to be calm and steady. 'Is that your definition of being neurotic? And assuming you're right about how I felt, are you trying to say no one should fight any battles with themselves?'

'Of course not,' he said on a contemptuous note. 'But I

am saying you're neurotic when you aren't honest with yourself. And I'm pretty sure you're not being honest.' She gasped at the unfairness of the attack, but he went on ruthlessly. 'In fact it's worse—with you. You're also not prepared to take anyone else's side of the story into account, not even prepared to listen, are you, Morgan?'

How *could* I listen? she thought torturedly. How could he explain it? No words are going to rub Sheila out like a magic eraser.

She jumped as he stood up unexpectedly and strode over to the railing. 'In fact dealing with you is like dealing with a brick wall, Morgan,' he said flatly.

'What's that supposed to mean?' she demanded fiercely, and thought, I may have regrets, but I'm not going to lie down and take all this like some dead fish!

'It means,' he said coolly, 'that assuming I'm right, and let us not *admit* anything,' he added cynically, 'assuming I'm right, if you were half human you could come to me and say look, my body tells me one thing but my head tells me another and I can't quite reconcile the two. But no, that would never do for Glamorgan Jones, would it?' he said ironically. 'Not she! Because on the basis of two unfortunate experiences, she's firmly convinced that all men are either exactly like her father or two inebriated kids she once had the misfortune to tangle with.'

'Are you . . . you're surely not trying to vindicate them?' she spluttered.

'You see,' he said scathingly, 'there you go again. No, I'm not trying to vindicate them—in fact you're deliberately missing the point. But would it hurt if you vindicated them? I mean, it was five years ago and you're still a virgin, I presume. Not only that, you're intelligent, in fact you're more, you're bloody bright! But not bright enough to know that I'm not like those two baboons or your father. That if you told me your heart does strange things when we get too close or that your breasts feel as if they were made to be cupped in my hands, I wouldn't immediately and automatically lead you down a pathway to hell.'

They stared at each other across the deck, their eyes locked and the air almost crackling with the tension between them.

Morgan licked her lips, but if it was as if there was a padlock on her heart and tongue to which she'd lost the key. A padlock that had less to do with her father and that unfortunate incident she'd suffered than he realised, and more to do with Sheila's unwitting revelation that Steven Harrow could ever realise. Yet it was still with a terrible feeling of desolation that she lowered her eyes in confusion—a confusion she couldn't hide.

He turned away from her at last and said bleakly, 'That's why I used the word neurotic, Morgan. But you're welcome to speak in your own defence.'

She tried to frame the words, tried desperately, but the image of a dozen pale mauve carnations kept intervening as they lay brokenly in the corners of her lounge room. The image of torn pages scattering to fall like snowflakes. And the final underlying image of herself perhaps visiting her successor and being unable, as Sheila had been, to control her emotions.

And all she could say finally was, 'I owe you some money. Will you let me repay it?'

'I don't want your money, Morgan.'

'But you must!' she insisted.

'Why must I? I know full well you're lying about the medical benefits. If you'd been conscious to make the choice, you'd have put yourself into a public ward—but you weren't. I made the choice. And if I do admit some small responsibility for you, it's that the staircase is a little hazardous . . . besides which, aren't you working for me because you're in some financial difficulty? How *would* you propose to pay me, just as a matter of interest?'

She hesitated. 'I don't know how you know all this, but you couldn't have known it at the time. So why should you bear the brunt of the expense because I happened to fall down your stairs? How *do* you know, by the way?'

'I checked with all the medical benefit funds,' he said baldly. 'But you haven't answered my question.'

'I was going to sell my car,' she said hastily, putting into words a shadowy thought. But while she'd thought it, she had also hoped she could offer to pay him in instalments from her salary.

A sneaky desire to leave some slender thread of communication open, Morgan? she asked herself. I wonder why?

She looked away from his mocking eyes as she said without thinking, 'Why ... did you make all those enquiries?'

Steve smiled coldly. 'Let's say I visualised having this conversation with you, my dear. Also, I'm not a philanthropist—at least not towards medical benefit companies.'

'But you're prepared to be one towards me. Why?' she asked, her voice thickening painfully. 'To make me feel for ever in your debt?' She regretted the words as soon as she'd uttered them, but there was no taking them back.

'Is that what you really think?' he asked after a long moment during which his blue eyes raked her mercilessly. She sat frozen. 'Well, I'm afraid that's just too bad. You'll have to learn to live with it, because whatever you happen to think my motives are, I won't be party to you selling your car. I suppose you do realise you could sue me?' he added negligently.

Morgan jumped up. 'You've accused me of being neurotic and ... inhuman and having a prejudiced view of men—and God knows what else. But do you honestly think I'd stoop to that? It never entered my head!'

He laughed then and moved forward to tower over her.

'Well, think about it, Morgan. Let your mind work around it,' he said softly. 'I'm sure it wouldn't be long before you decided that not only do I want you in my debt for ever but I'm also doing it to keep you sweet in case you should decide to sue for damages.'

'Oh, I hate you,' she said clearly. 'You're deliberately making me out to be a ... to be ... and all because I won't go to bed with you! You're punishing me, aren't you? Is it any wonder Sheila is quite para. ...' She broke off in a panic as he caught hold of one of her wrists.

'My, my,' he said casually. 'What a temper! And why bring Sheila up now?' he added, echoing her own desperate thoughts. 'I thought you'd closed your ears on the subject,' he went on. 'Don't tell me you're turning her into a weapon to use against me? I might have known!'

He dropped her wrist and turned away with a gesture of disgust.

Oh, you're so clever, Mr Harrow, Morgan thought dully. You can out-talk me so often. But I can't ... I just can't accept it!

'Look,' she said, on the edge of tears, 'let's agree to differ, shall we? Let's admit we have no common ground and perhaps I'm the one at fault ... anyway,' she said brokenly, and shrugged dispiritedly, 'I must pay you back somehow. I may be wrong to do it, but I have to.'

She fixed her eye on one of his shirt buttons and noted vaguely that it seemed to be moving in and out rather quickly. I've made him really angry, she thought miserably. But I can't seem to help it.

She tensed as she felt his fingers beneath her chin and resisted for a moment before allowing him to raise it so she had to look into his eyes. And what she saw in those eyes, as they travelled slowly over her, puzzled her. All the anger seemed to have drained away, to be replaced by something she couldn't put a name to—except to know that it was no longer anything violent.

And his next words confirmed this.

He said meditatively, 'All right, but I don't want your money. I have more than enough of my own. You'll have to think of some other way of paying me.'

Her mind raced furiously. What did he mean? Surely not. . . . But the sudden glint of humour in his eyes seemed to taunt her and she reddened.

'No, my dear, I don't mean that,' he said softly.

'I can't think of anything,' she said unsteadily. 'What's wrong with me paying you something out of my salary every week?'

'Morgan,' he said slowly, 'as I said before, your few dollars a week don't really attract me. But if you really want to repay me, there is one way you could do it. Unfortunately it's probably the one way that wouldn't appeal to you. If you were to continue as my research secretary. . . .'

'That's crazy,' she said lamely at last. 'I mean, after all the labels you've stuck on me this morning, I would have thought I'd be the last person you'd want to have around. I mean, I'd have been an idiot not to gather that you despised me totally.'

'Don't "gather" anything about me, Morgan,' he said hardly. 'And there is one area in which you excel. I could never find anyone else—on a part-time basis—who could equal you as a secretary and an editor. As a matter of fact, so far as grammar goes, I only regret not having the use of you earlier. You have an almost Churchillian way of pruning my more extravagant sentences. In fact you're the essence of what Anatole France meant when he said you become a good writer just as you become a good joiner, by planing down your sentence. In that respect, we make a very good team and you're worth your weight in gold, my dear Morgan.'

'I . . . I. . . .' she stammered.

'You mean you're not serious about repaying me,

Morgan?' he said softly but with a bite in his voice.

She found she couldn't answer.

Steve studied her hot face. 'Let's say on half-pay, shall we?' Then he turned away uninterestedly to add over his shoulder with a shrug, 'You might as well accept it, Morgan. Because if you don't you'll find yourself being bundled into your little car and that's the last you'll ever see of me.'

The silence grew.

He turned back to her at last. 'And then you'd have to live with the thought of my charity for ever.'

Bother Churchill, she found herself thinking unexpectedly. Blow him! And Anatole France, she added irrationally. And what of me? I should be jumping up and down for joy because I've finally got through to Steve Harrow. My secretarial skills have won the day and I've effectively killed any attraction that might have been there stone dead. Why else wouldn't he be wishing me on the other side of the moon? But do I feel like rejoicing?

No. Not me. Not Glamorgan Jones. She feels as if she was going to a funeral. Which just goes to show what a sublime idiot she is.

But at least Sheila can rest in peace.

Morgan was welcomed back at work enthusiastically by one and all. And before her first day back ended, she began to feel as if her two weeks off had been an illusion.

It was also at the end of her first day that she realised Ryan was not quite his usual perky self. This was confirmed when he noticed her looking at him once and immediately an almost guarded expression came into his eyes.

Morgan took the hint that day, but several days later couldn't contain herself any longer.

'What is it, Ryan?' she asked as they shared a hurried lunch.

'What's what?' he countered.

'Listen, Ryan,' she said gently but with a not quite hidden note of steel, 'you dragged all my secrets out of me. Don't think I won't do the same to you! So you'd better come clean and tell me why you're getting around like a lovesick Romeo. . . .' She stopped abruptly. 'Is *that* it?' she asked, suddenly enlightened. 'Have you fallen in love at last?'

He grimaced and shrugged. 'Call it what you like,' he said slowly. 'All I know is, it's a lost cause if ever there was one.'

'But why?' Morgan asked. 'Is she married?'

'Nope,' he said briefly.

'I don't believe it!' she said after a long pause. 'What happened to all your optimism? Remember all the advice you gave me? You seemed to be so sure there was no such thing as a lost cause!'

'Well, there is,' he said baldly. 'And I was wrong. And if you knew her, you'd agree with me. In fact you do, though I can't imagine why you choose not to let on.'

'I know her?' Morgan said bewilderedly, casting around in her mind for all their mutual acquaintances. 'You don't mean the little girl from the bank?'

'No, Morgan, I don't,' said Ryan a little grimly. 'It's someone right out of her league—and mine, I guess. It's Sheila Somerville.'

Morgan's mouth dropped open and her eyes widened incredulously.

'Yes,' Ryan agreed bitterly. 'Now, do you want to tell me again it's not a lost cause?'

'But . . . but,' Morgan stammered, 'you've only met her once. . . .'

'Three times,' Ryan said gloomily. 'She came in very early one morning to get your address.' Morgan started. Ryan went on unnoticing. 'And then she came in last week to make those bookings. I . . . it was just before closing time and I persuaded her to have a drink with me.'

Morgan digested this slowly. 'How come . . . I mean, if she's going away with Steve Harrow why did she have a drink with you? I mean. . . .'

'I don't know the answer to that one either, Morgan,' he shrugged, 'but she was very tense. And you know me, I always reckon there's no harm in asking.'

'What . . . what did she tell you?' Morgan asked jerkily.

'As a matter of fact, she asked me a whole lot of questions about you. Which I kind of anticipated, fortunately, having almost fallen off my chair when she made the bookings in the name of Somerville and Harrow. Mr S. Harrow . . . by the way, why did she want your address?'

'She . . . she came to see me,' Morgan said painfully. 'She . . . got very upset, I'm afraid. I. . . .'

'I was afraid of that,' Ryan remarked. 'She's head over heels in love with the guy, isn't she? I must say he's got to be quite a bloke. I mean he's got not one, but two of the most gorgeous girls I know in tow. I wish to hell he'd either make up his mind or break a leg, preferably both of them!' he added surprisingly viciously.

'Ryan,' Morgan said slowly, '. . . incidentally, he hasn't got me in tow, but I don't suppose that's much consolation to you, but do you really like her? She's an awful snob, you know.'

Ryan smiled suddenly and reached out to place a finger lightly on Morgan's lips. 'Honey,' he said gently, 'she's insanely jealous of you. You can't expect her to act reasonably, now can you? She's all woman.'

Morgan bit her lip and they exchanged a rueful look.

'I don't mean you're not,' Ryan added hastily. 'But. . . .'

'That's all right, I know what you mean,' Morgan said wryly. 'So spare me the explanations, please. I've had enough of those to last me a lifetime. But listen, Ryan,' she tried once more, 'three meetings? Isn't that rather soon to fall in love?'

He lifted his shoulders. 'Who knows? All *I* know is that I can't get her out of my mind. How long did it take you to fall in love with Steve Harrow?'

The picture that flashed into Morgan's mind then was devastatingly accurate, for all that it depicted a scene that had been and gone for longer than five years. It was a lecture room and the arrival of the new geography lecturer. And herself, looking up as he entered the room and catching her breath as she saw him for the first time.

She lowered her eyes and couldn't think of anything to say at all.

It was Ryan who said quizzically, 'Now if you were to accept my advice, about Steve Harrow, Morgan, I might be in with a chance. I don't suppose you feel like telling me what's been going on since we last discussed the subject?'

'Nothing,' Morgan said stoically. 'I'm sorry, Ryan, but if anything it's all the more impossible now.'

'Is it?' he queried with a faint tinge of disbelief as he studied her averted face. 'Haven't you seen him?'

'Yes, I have, and I'll still be working for him—but that's all,' she said as firmly as she could.

'And still be in love with, won't you? You don't fool me, Morgan. I don't think you've fooled anyone.'

'All right, Ryan,' Morgan said tartly. 'I may not have. To be quite honest I don't give a damn! But in the light of what you now know about Sheila Somerville, surely even you must realise it's not as simple as it might have once appeared to you? I know . . . look, I'm sorry, but I know he's sleeping with her. Or was very recently. Isn't it then quite reasonable to suppose that if he can toss her out to make room for me, some day he'd do the same to me?'

'Did he ever try to . . . take you to bed? Forcibly, I mean? Take unfair advantage of you?'

Morgan exhaled slowly. 'If you mean did he try to seduce me, yes, he did. All the time I was with him it was sort of there, if you know what I mean. But he could have . . . at least. . . .' She broke off in confusion.

'If he could have but he didn't—that's a plus, surely,' Ryan said thoughtfully. 'Perhaps he was too clever for that . . . I wonder?'

'There's no need to wonder any more, Ryan. It's over. I'm *sorry*—but it's a fact.'

And those were the last words they spoke on the subject for quite some time, although Morgan couldn't suppress a trickle of unease at the faraway look in Ryan's eyes.

Nor could she suppress a start of surprise when she noticed by accident that the dates for the Lord Howe trip coincided with the school vacation and Brad Smith's much talked of safari into the interior with Steve Harrow. But she closed her mind firmly and refused to even speculate on this.

And for reasons of his own, Ryan didn't tell her when he received a phone call cancelling the Lord Howe trip.

CHAPTER EIGHT

MORGAN stared pensively into space and then back at her desk calendar. It was roughly two and a half months since she'd plunged over Steve Harrow's spiral staircase, she noted, and for some reason, sighed deeply. Two and a half months, she thought, of hell!

Not that I can deny that our business arrangement isn't working very well, because it is. Too well, because anything less loverlike than Steve Harrow would be hard to imagine, she thought dismally. Always nice, always thoughtful, sometimes funny, especially when he and Brad get together, but not even a glimmer of anything personal. And it's half killing me, she acknowledged with a tiny, wry quirk to her lips. I thought I could do it, but I have to admit I'll be very glad when this book is finished. Or will I?

Yes, I will, she told herself brusquely. And gave herself a mental shake.

But two minutes later she couldn't prevent her thoughts from returning once more to the subject. If only I knew—how Sheila's fared. . . .

She glanced obliquely at Ryan, working steadily beside her. I wonder if he knows? But if I ask him that'll be an open invitation to dig up the past, and I don't particularly want that. Besides, she thought, for a man who thought himself so in love, Ryan seems to have recovered remarkably quickly too. In fact I'm almost sure he's bounced right back—to use his own words, or were they mine?

But she found throughout that very busy Monday that her own thoughts kept returning to plague her. Had

Ryan recovered completely?

And now that Steve and Brad are away on their field trip and you feel so desperately lonely, how do you imagine you're going to cope when the book is finished and you won't have any excuse for seeing him again, Morgan?

And did Sheila go away with them?

'Dear God! I wish I knew,' she muttered fiercely beneath her breath. 'I feel as if I'm in a cage going round and round on a treadmill! I also wish I hadn't been quite so obstinate and determined to shut Ryan up. At least I'd have some idea of what was going on!'

Fortunately for her the pressure of work began to make itself felt at that point and she surrendered to it.

School vacations annually saw a stream of Southern Australians head for Queensland beaches, and never more so than during the winter months. And many a Queenslander born and bred who actually felt cold during these months marvelled at their tough, pale southern neighbours who got around scantily clad and, worse, actually swam at this time of year.

But Morgan's more immediate problems were the numbers of them who flocked into the agency seeking sightseeing information or alterations to their bookings at a rate that kept her and Ryan flat out and even caused their manager to mutter about employing extra staff.

'I wish he'd do it instead of just talking about it,' said Ryan vehemently late that afternoon. 'This pace is even beginning to tell on my love-life!'

Morgan grinned at that. 'Dear me,' she murmured. 'That would be disastrous, wouldn't it? But this happens every year, Ryan. I mean that he talks about it and does nothing. Perhaps you should put yourself on layby for a while. You know, ration your love-life a little.' This was, she found, the closest she could come to asking him about Sheila.

But he chose not to accept the bait. He said wryly,

'Tut-tut, Morgan. I see you haven't lost your nasty way with words. Layby, eh? How's *your* love-life going, by the way? Still non-existent?'

She flashed him a speaking look and he pretended to duck, but with a grin on his face, and picked up his phone.

And when he replaced it, it was with an expression quite akin to the cat who'd caught the canary.

Morgan raised her eyebrows enquiringly at him.

He grinned a little sheepishly. 'That bird on Qantas reservations. You know, the one with the gravelly voice?'

Morgan nodded. 'Don't tell me she's accepted a date with you?'

'Yes, she has,' he said complacently. 'All it takes is a bit of patience, you know, Morgan,' he added loftily.

'Have you seen her?' Morgan asked with two thoughts in mind, one of them being that perhaps here was the answer to her question.

'Don't need to,' Ryan replied. 'Her voice says it all. Besides, airlines don't go in for chicks what ain't lookers. You know that, Morgan! What is it?' he added at her expression.

'Nothing,' she said hastily. 'When is this momentous meeting?'

'Tonight after work.' He named a hotel in town. 'For drinks. You look peculiar, Morgan. Why is that, I wonder?'

'Peculiar. You mean funny peculiar or funny ha-ha?' she asked innocently.

'I wish I knew,' he said pensively. 'By the way, how's *your* love-life, love?'

'Non-existent,' she said airily, refusing to be ruffled.

'Still working for him?'

'Yes—well, not at the moment. He's away on a field trip. But he's due back any day.' She pulled a stack of files towards her as she spoke.

'Is he now! How long has he been away?'

Long enough, Morgan thought. But she said, 'A few weeks. Ryan, if you don't start doing something now, you might have to work late tonight, friend.'

This had the desired effect, although he shot her a keen, amused glance as he swung his chair round. 'Say no more, Morgan!' he commanded. 'Not that you were going to anyway,' he added half to himself. 'Back to the galley, slave!' He reached for a file. 'My lips are sealed!'

'Good!' she retorted. 'Let's hope they stay that way for a while.'

'Er . . . Morgan? Hey!' he protested and ducked as she turned to him with a flashing look. 'I was merely going to ask you,' he said with an injured air, 'how the devil does one arrange for a family of seven to meet a crocodile?'

'Send them to Cairns,' she said promptly. 'I believe the place abounds with them. And what's more, they're getting quite saucy. Developing a taste for man.'

'Is that so? Funny, I've been to Cairns, but I've never met one. Are you having me on?'

'No. Well—a little, but I was reading about it in the paper the other day. I thought *you* were having *me* on?'

'I'm not,' he said with a snort. 'Don't you remember that mad family that wanted to know where they could buy a live koala? And take it home to America as a pet? Well, now they're into crocodiles!'

For some reason Morgan found herself chuckling about this on and off during the day and again as she parked her car neatly in her garage. She didn't notice the battered Land Rover parked in the street, but she was still smiling to herself as she fitted her key into the door and was nearly bowled over by Brad Smith as he came up behind her and gave her an enthusiastic bear-hug.

'Brad!' she said laughingly as she bent to retrieve her handbag. 'You're back. Did you have a good time?'

'First class, Morgan! It was beaut. Only thing, it wasn't long enough!' he replied energetically, and removed his large foot from her sunglasses which he'd stood on inadvertently. 'Hey, Morgan! I think . . . no, they're not broken. Why do sheilas always carry so much clobber in their purses?'

'I sometimes wonder that myself,' she said ruefully as they picked up the last few miscellaneous objects. 'It just seems to accumulate. There. Now let me look at you, Brad. I do believe you've grown! In fact I think you're taller than I am now!'

He shrugged offhandedly. 'I couldn't have grown in three weeks. But I do feel as if I've stretched a bit,' He reddened slightly. 'I had the best time I've ever had in my life,' he said seriously. 'And it's all thanks to you, Morgan.'

'Me?' she protested. 'Don't be silly, Brad. I had nothing to do with it.'

'Yes, you did. If you hadn't got yourself the best shiner in town, I'd never have really got to know the guy!' he said eagerly.

Morgan laughed helplessly. 'Well, I'm glad to have been of service, Brad. Er . . . where is the guy, by the way?' she managed to say without any sign of a tremor in her voice. 'I suppose he dropped you off and went home?'

'Nah. He stopped off to say hello to Mum and she made him stay and have a cup of tea. But he'll be over to see you as soon as he can get away, I guess. I'm going to tell him you're home. See you later, Morgan. Boy, have I got lots to tell my mates!'

'Brad. . . .'

But if he heard her, he took no notice and strode away.

Morgan bit her lip and let herself into the flat with a feeling akin to panic. What I need is a drink, she thought, and poured herself one with shaking hands. But why do I feel this way? I've seen him once a week for the past three months almost—until they went away—without shaking and carrying on like a star-struck schoolgirl. I'd even begun to believe that I'd achieved my own inoculation. I really thought I'd got my life back on to a steady even keel. .

And if I realised that Steve Harrow would always represent a scar or a wound, at least I knew the pain was fading. Yes, fading, Morgan, she reminded herself, but perhaps never to fade completely.

I know, she answered herself, but at least I proved I could live with it.

She swirled the liquid in her glass. 'So why do I feel like this?' she murmured out aloud. 'Why . . .?'

A light tattoo on her door made her start convulsively. She stared around wildly for a moment and then deliberately pulled herself together. She put her glass down out of sight behind a vase and flicked her hair back with her forefingers. Then she crossed to the door, opened it—and took a deep breath. And for the first few moments all she saw were his eyes. Those blue, blue eyes staring into her own, unsmilingly and peculiarly intent.

She licked her lips unconsciously and stepped back a pace as if to lessen the impact of his gaze. 'Come in,' she said with the muscles of her throat feeling stiff. She dropped her eyes and sought for just the right note as she said, 'You look as if you've grown too!' and immediately thought, now why on earth did I say that? But it was true. He seemed taller and his shoulders broader than she remembered them.

'Unless,' she went on, aware that she was getting in deeper but unable to stop, 'unless I've shrunk!' she said with a totally false brightness.

She winced inwardly and turned away. 'Would you . . . would you like a drink?' She looked back over her shoulder enquiringly and wondered if it was her imagination or whether he did seem to relax visibly.

Steve said with a grin as he shoved his hands into the pockets of his dusty khaki trousers, 'Actually I would.' He strolled into the lounge and looked around. 'I'm awash with sweet milky tea. Something with a bit of bite in it would be most welcome.'

He turned suddenly and they almost bumped into each other.

'Excuse me,' Morgan said hastily, and went to move past him, but he put out a restraining hand to detain her.

'There's no rush,' he said wryly. 'How are you, anyway? You look thinner.'

'Do I? I hadn't noticed,' she tried to say lightly as he held her out at arm's length and looked her up and down with his eyes slightly narrowed. 'Perhaps I'm working too hard,' she went on, unnerved by the feel of his hand on her arm and his thoughtful scrutiny. 'We've been really busy these past few weeks. Ryan never stops grumbling. He even says. . . .' She stopped abruptly and felt the colour flood her face.

'Even says what?'

'Er . . . says it interferes with his love-life,' she mumbled, and pulled away.

Steve raised his eyebrows quizzically. 'I feel for Ryan,' he said, his eyes sparkling with amusement.

Morgan turned and moved towards the cupboard where she kept a lone bottle of brandy. 'Will this do?' She held the bottle out for his inspection. 'I'm afraid it's all I have.'

'Admirably. Is *your* love-life suffering, Morgan?'

Well, I asked for that, didn't I? she thought philosophically, and was amazed to find that all her nerves and jitters had suddenly deserted her. Perhaps fielding that question twice in one day has done it, she mused as she poured him a drink.

She shrugged and handed him the glass. 'You can't damage something that's non-existent, can you? But I'm afraid your book has suffered a little. I had hoped to have it right up to date by the time you came back.'

'Don't worry about it. I'm sure you've done well. Aren't you going to join me?' he queried as he sat down and raised his glass.

Morgan hesitated and then reached behind the vase for her drink. 'In fact I'm ahead of you,' she told him, and sat down herself.

'Brad. . . .'

'I. . . .'

They spoke simultaneously and both smiled. 'Go on,' he said smoothly.

'I was going to say Brad looks like a different kid.' She traced the rim of her glass with her forefinger.

'I hope so. He's all set to go on and get his senior certificate now and go to university.'

'Don't tell me he's caught the bug?'

He lifted his shoulders and said wryly, 'Maybe. Personally I think he'll end up being an engineer if he sticks at it. He certainly exhibited an aptitude for it. But at least he's thinking now, not just existing from one bout of mischief to the next. He . . . er . . . tells me he won't be wagging any more tutoring sessions with you, by the way.'

Morgan raised her eyebrows. 'Heaven help me,' she commented. 'If he's going to be as dedicated a student as he was a slacker I might be in for a busy time!'

Steve grinned. 'I know what you mean. All that energy can be quite exhausting. Morgan, why did you let me think you got paid for helping these kids?'

'Did I?' she said lightly after a moment. 'Yes, I did, I remember now. I suppose it was a kind of defence mechanism. I didn't want you feeling sorry for me and I didn't particularly want your job at that time. Why do you ask?'

'Well,' he moved a hand sideways. 'how can I explain it? It made me think that accumulating money was very important to you somehow. I. . . .'

'But it is,' she interrupted seriously. 'I suffer from a feeling of insecurity without it. I think most people do, probably. But I don't think I'm totally mercenary. Do you?'

His lashes were lowered as he contemplated his drink and he didn't reply for a long moment. Then he said equally seriously, still without looking at her, 'I must confess that in days gone by I did cherish the nasty thought that the only way I would get you to go to bed with me would be to offer to pay you. Now don't hit me, Morgan,' he added quizzically as she gasped. 'I know we vowed to close that subject for ever, but I thought since we'd been so successful in . . . in defusing our relationship, I could admit it and offer to apologise.' He looked up and across at her, his blue eyes sparkling intimately in a way that quite took her breath away.

'Apology accepted,' she said gruffly when she finally found her voice.

'But you know, I'm still curious,' he said with his head to one side. 'About how you came to be in that position, that slight financial jam. Won't you enlighten me?'

She stood up. 'It was . . . let's just say it was money well spent.' She closed her eyes briefly and wondered why she couldn't bring herself to tell him about her father. *Maybe I'm not that proud of that gesture*, she thought with a sudden flash of insight. *I should have gone to him as well. The money could have stretched. After all, he's getting old and he was very ill. I should have. I will go*, she thought with suddenly clenched fists. *As soon as I've saved up enough money, I will. Somehow or other I'll scrape it together. . . .*

Steve's hand on her shoulder interrupted her reverie. 'What is it?' he asked gently as her eyes flew upwards. 'You look as if you're in pain almost.'

'Nothing,' she said unsteadily. 'I'm all right. I was just

so busy today I didn't get a chance to have lunch.'

His eyes searched her face. 'I wish I could believe you,' he said quietly. 'But I don't. You're not . . . going through the same thing you went through with me, with some other man, are you, Morgan? Is that what's making you look so tortured?'

'No, of course not! I mean, we're back to all those old assumptions, aren't we?'

'Are we? I thought we agreed to differ. But whichever, is that what it is, Morgan? Some man?'

'No! I . . . oh *yes!* It is, but not what you think. . . .'

She broke off and gasped as his fingers tightened cruelly on her shoulder, then he dropped his hand suddenly and moved away.

'So? What's the problem?' he asked in a curiously contained voice. 'As one who's been through it, I might be able to offer some advice. Is he finding this platonic business rather rough going? Or have you finally decided that a meeting of the minds is not the only thing that brings two people together truly?'

'It's nothing like that,' she said through her teeth, now thoroughly infuriated as much by his unquestioning assumptions as his sardonic tone of voice. 'And it's none of your business either,' she added coldly.

'Ah, but it is,' he said softly yet with a dangerous glint in his eye. 'As an anthropologist I find it fascinating. Human behaviour in the raw. I could almost find a place for you in my thesis, my dear Morgan. . . .'

'Get out!' she spat at him. 'Get out this instant before I throw you out. How *dare* you!'

But he threw his head back and laughed. 'Why don't you try it?' he invited with a lingering smile that was insufferably superior and taunting.

And just the last straw to Morgan as she launched herself at him, intent on wiping it off his face if it was the last thing she did and totally lost to all reason in her fury.

But her hands never reached his face, because with a
swift, effortless movement he caught her wrists and im-
prisoned them behind her back in a grasp of steel.

She struggled desperately, her breath coming in uneven
gasps, but his arms were like iron bands around her own
and her body was ruthlessly jammed against his so that
she could feel the outline of his strong hard thighs against
her own as he bent her backwards. But the pain in her
wrenched back shoulder-blades was accompanied by
other sensations she didn't dare name yet couldn't ignore.
And it was with a long shuddering sigh that she gave up
the unequal struggle and slumped in his arms like a
broken reed with her hair lying across his arm and her
upturned face like a pale flower as the colour ebbed.

'There,' he said a little indistinctly, and released her
wrists to slip his arms about her waist as she sagged against
him. 'I'll never understand you, Morgan. You have all the
weapons any woman could wish for, but you're just not
capable of using them!' His blue gaze slid over her pale
features with an almost brooding quality. 'What you need
is a lesson in loving before you drive some man to distrac-
tion!'

Her eyes widened as he picked her up and carried her
to the settee with one of her arms swinging lifelessly. He
put her down so that she was half sitting, half lying, and
sat down beside her. Then with an impatient gesture at
the way she crumpled bonelessly into the cushions he
gathered her into his arms again.

'What we need to do is break down the barriers,
Morgan,' he said roughly. 'Like this.' He unbuttoned her
blouse with sure fingers and then undid the clasp of her
bra and she trembled at the feel of his strong warm fingers
playing lightly on her spine. But her eyes remained fixed
and distended.

Steve frowned and she trembled again at the look of
barely contained violence in his eyes as those exploring

fingers slid downwards to the waistband of her skirt and then moved round her waist as if emphasising its slenderness. She tensed, but realised immediately that she had made the wrong move, because she saw his pupils contract as he felt her gather herself beneath his hands.

She breathed deeply in an effort to force herself to relax, but it was too late. He sat her upright but still within the circle of one arm, and despite each somehow boneless movement of resistance she made, he carefully removed her blouse and bra.

He said with a nerve beating in his jaw, 'I never thought I'd resort to bodice-ripping, Glamorgan, but I'm sure it's in a good cause. You know, what you don't realise in your splendid and enforced isolation,' his eyes flicked contemptuously over her face, 'is that in a loving situation it's what you give that counts. If you could give some man joy without—for once—worrying about yourself and your inhibitions and your hang-ups, there's no way you can come away poorer from the experience. And this,' he said, his voice deepened and rough again, 'is how you do it.'

She closed her eyes languidly as those seeking fingers found her breasts, cupping and plucking gently but insistently until her nipples hardened and peaked and she thought she might die from the exquisite sensations she felt through her whole body from her scalp that prickled, rhythmically, to her toes.

'Because that's the basis of a true relationship. This,' he went on relentlessly with his lips against her throat. 'If you give all this to a man, willingly and eagerly and unselfishly, you earn in return the key to their souls.'

Morgan moaned within her throat as his lips and tongue explored the tender skin behind her ear lobes, and then returned to her lips to tease them apart while his free hand cupped and roamed the swell of her breasts at will.

It was a mind-bending kiss that seemed to last for ever—at least until she was arching her body across his lap in a fervour of desire, uncaring for once as she never had been before.

At last his lips left hers. And at last she knew she couldn't deny herself the luxury of touching him. Of running her fingers through his hair. Of spreading her palms across his shoulder blades beneath his shirt. But as the thought transmitted itself to deed, she was arrested as he spoke again.

'And then, my dear Morgan, when you have the key to their souls, then you can commune mentally, which is what you're crying out for—do you think I don't know that?'

Her hand hovered and clenched because of something in his voice, some note of discord.

'Do you think I don't know it?' he said again, barely audibly, his eyes raking her before they closed briefly. 'But you can't have one without the other. Not truly, Glamorgan. So when you go to this man, remember what your old lecturer told you, won't you? You used to accept my word as gospel in those days. Accept it now.' He released her and sat her up primly against the corner cushions of the settee. 'I've met—for research purposes and otherwise,' he said gravely, 'women who aren't brilliant or educated but are nevertheless warm, and loving, and you'd be surprised at the admiration, respect—indeed, worship they've earned from their menfolk. And you'd be surprised at the basic wisdom they've exhibited. They'd leave you for dead, my dear. So think on it all, Morgan.' He reached for her blouse which was on the floor at his feet and used it to cover her nakedness ineffectually.

'Take another view of it for once,' he said grimly as he rose to his feet. 'Wonder if you aren't pricing yourself out of the market, sweetheart. The market of living, breathing people. Not puppets, not cyphers. There's only one way to cure yourself, Glamorgan. I've just proved to you you're not frigid—let this man prove the rest, if you dare.'

She twisted her head and looked with stricken eyes as he moved away towards the front door.

He stopped and turned to cast a strangely impersonal glance over her. 'But then again,' he said on a gently satirical note, 'I've never denied that you're a good research secretary—one of the best. Maybe they could write that on your gravestone?' He chewed his knuckle and thought for a moment. 'Yes, how would this sound?

Here lies Glamorgan Jones,
A secretary beyond compare,
A typist—who was never really there.
A robot in fact, but did she exist?
No.
No, just an entry in the Births and Deaths List. . . .'

Morgan felt her jaw sag beneath this cruel onslaught. But it was not finished, she realised as he added by way of a parting shot,

'By the way, I told Brad you were coming up this Saturday and you'd give him a lift. So I guess I'll see you then? If not your shadow.'

And so saying, he closed the front door gently behind him.

If Morgan was heavy-eyed from lack of sleep the following morning and moving around rather like a wan ghost, Ryan was equally preoccupied, she noticed thankfully through the fog of her own misery.

And something on the outer edge of her mind . . . something to do with Ryan, she thought fleetingly, was bothering her. But she couldn't put her finger on it and gave herself over to the monumental task of trying to concentrate on her job.

So it was around mid-morning when they were both able to take a lightning coffee break at their desks before Ryan said to her reproachfully, 'You knew, didn't you, Morgan?'

His tone was so laden with an air of injury that she started with her coffee cup half way to her mouth and asked, 'Knew what? What are you talking about? What is it, Ryan?' she added more urgently as she turned to him and took in his air of deflation.

A sequence of probabilities flashed through her mind as he studiously avoided her concerned gaze. Could he have been given his notice? No. She rejected that out of hand. Her startled mind flew back to the large lady who had overheard his 'bottom-pinching' conversation. Maybe she had registered a very forceful complaint. Had Ryan been severely carpeted over the incident?

'For heaven's sake, Ryan,' she said at last in exasperation, 'what is it?'

'That innocent look doesn't fool me for a moment, Morgan,' he said at last with an expression of disdain. 'You knew she was engaged. Not just engaged,' he added irately, 'as if that wasn't bad enough,' he muttered, 'but,' he went on emphasising every word, 'engaged to a bloke who's six foot six and plays scrum-half in the Queensland Rugby Union side! You do realise he could have made mincemeat of me with one hand tied behind his back, don't you?' He glared at her.

'Oh, *Ryan*!' she exclaimed, enlightened at last and unable to contain a gurgle of laughter. 'You mean Jenny White from Qantas reservations? No, I didn't. I mean,' she amended, still struggling to keep a straight face, 'I did know she was engaged. I didn't realise he was so . . . so . . . formidable. Honestly, I had no idea!'

'But you were quite willing to allow me to be set up, Morgan? Totally embarrassed, made to look a real fool, not to mention about two foot high. . . .'

Morgan gave way to her mirth and put her hands over her ears. 'Don't say any more, Ryan,' she pleaded at last. 'I shall get a stitch!'

'Which is no more than you deserve you cruel, heartless. . . . Is that any way to treat a friend?' he demanded.

'Look,' she said with a giggle, 'I didn't have anything to do with it. The only thing I knew about it was when I was talking to Jenny one day and she said to me that you were the most persistent bloke she'd ever met. You just wouldn't take no for an answer. So I asked her if she'd told you she was engaged and she said no, why should she? Surely it was enough to say, as she did very politely, she assured me, that she wasn't interested in meeting you? But I must admit last night I did wonder if she was planning to teach you a lesson. Was it very bad?' she asked sympathetically but still with a grin on her face.

'Picture it if you can,' Ryan said gloomily. 'The place was crowded but I knew her straight away because of her uniform. So I waltzed up to her and boy! was I right about her being a looker. Anyway, she introduced me to this bozo who seemed to be hanging around, but I gave him short shrift because after all my weeks of hard work I had no intention of sharing her with anyone. But he still kept hanging round, so finally I told him to kick off. About one second later, I suddenly noticed this big diamond on her ring finger . . . matter of fact I noticed it just as the words left my mouth. Er . . . then it dawned on me who he was! Of all the unkind tricks, that had to be the lowest, I can tell you, Morgan!'

But Morgan was off again in a paroxysm of laughter. 'Oh dear,' she said as she wiped her eyes. 'What did he do?'

'Nothing,' Ryan said broodingly. 'Just looked me up and down and then had the gall to offer to buy me a drink.' He started to grin reluctantly and said, 'Didn't realise I was capable of back-pedalling so quickly. It was a sore blow to my ego, Morgan. I might never recover, do you realise that?' he added piously but with a twinkle of laughter in his eyes.

'Yes, you will, Ryan. Still, it might be an idea to be more cautious in future,' she replied promptly.

'I guess so. But there can't be that many six foot six scrum-halves around to monster me, can there, Morgan?'

'Now see, you've recovered already!' said Morgan, and chuckled again.

'Well,' he straightened and his face sobered suddenly, 'if you knew how wrong you were, Morgan. If you only knew. . . .'

'Knew what?' she said slowly, unable to fathom his expression and with a sudden feeling of unease.

There was a little silence. Finally he spoke with an uneven edge to his voice. 'Knew how much pain these antics of mine are designed to cover—and how little they cover it. Forgive me for presuming to offer you any advice, Morgan. I just didn't know . . . what it was really like.'

Morgan felt her eyes widen. 'Ryan. . . .' she whispered. 'I was so sure you'd got over Sheila!'

He grimaced and she winced at the sudden glimpse of pain in his eyes. 'The way I feel, I doubt if I ever will. But perhaps I don't have to tell you about that special feeling. I gather he's back?'

'Yes,' she said not quite steadily.

'I thought so. When you came in this morning you looked as if . . . as if you might never laugh again. Has he told you anything about Sheila?'

'No,' she whispered. 'Have you seen her?'

Ryan nodded. 'Quite a bit. She . . . I've been providing a shoulder to cry on. She got her marching orders, you see. Apparently it came to a head over the Lord Howe trip. She hadn't consulted him when she made the bookings.'

'I didn't know,' said Morgan with a barely concealed

tremor in her voice. 'I mean I realised they weren't going to the Island. I . . . I thought she might have gone camping with them.'

Ryan lifted his brows. 'I reckon she would have even done that, if he'd asked her.' He shrugged wearily. 'There's—I don't know, but I get this feeling that until he *marries* someone, she's not going to give up on him either—in her heart, that is. There's some very strong bond that she can't seem to break.'

Morgan closed her eyes and felt tears on her lashes. But she said, 'I hope you're not recommending me for the position, Ryan. I'd love to be able to do it for you . . . that sounds crazy, but . . . anyway. . . .' she faltered and trailed off helplessly.

'And I can't deny I'd love to be able to arrange it for her sake,' he said quietly. 'Even if I didn't benefit in the long run. Which just goes to show,' he added with an attempt at flippancy that didn't quite come off, 'what true love does to one.'

'Maybe she'll come round without it,' Morgan said tentatively. 'She must like you or she wouldn't have told you all this. Perhaps with time?'

'Perhaps,' he said, and turned away, looking more vulnerable than she'd ever thought possible for Ryan.

CHAPTER NINE

For the rest of the week Morgan found herself in possibly a worse dilemma than usual. The thought of Sheila's plight increased her sense of injury towards Steve Harrow if anything, and she kept seeing that beautiful, distraught face again. And this, coupled with the still simmering anger at the way her employer had treated her on the last occasion they had met, combined to lead her to an abrupt decision late one evening as she typed speedily on *his* typewriter which she had brought home so that she could continue working on his manuscript while he and Brad were away.

And it was with a sigh that she laid the last corrected page on top of the pile and stretched wearily. Then she stared down at the two hundred or so pages with unseeing eyes.

'That's it,' she murmured. 'I've paid off my debt. I don't have to see him again and I don't intend to. The only problem . . .' she broke off and chewed one finger-tip meditatively, 'is how to get his typewriter back to him. And how to explain to Brad that I won't be going on Saturday.'

She closed her eyes and sighed heavily. What a mess! she thought. Her mind slipped back involuntarily to that last disastrous meeting. What a nerve he has, she thought, and felt a flame of anger lick through her as she remembered his little verse.

And he was quite happy to accuse me of not even being prepared to listen to his explanations about Sheila, but would he listen to me? Oh no!

And she was still angry the next morning, as Ryan discovered.

'Seen Harrow again?' he queried, seemingly idly.

'No!' she snapped at him. 'And I don't intend to.'

He raised his eyebrows. 'So you're not working for him any more? Have you left him in the lurch?'

'No,' she said through her teeth. 'I've worked my fingers to the bone for him this week, as it happens. It's just a matter of getting the stuff up to him. . . .' She trailed off at the sudden alert look in Ryan's eyes. 'Why are you looking like that?' she asked warily.

He shrugged. 'Am I? I don't know. Does that mean he's not yet aware you've sworn off him?'

She tightened her lips and refused to speak.

'If you tell me, Morgan,' he said cajolingly, 'I'll tell you about the crazy plans I've been nurturing this week.'

She eyed him unpleasantly. 'I knew you were up to something! All right, you go first.'

'See,' Ryan said cautiously. 'it did occur to me that he might be the one who needed the shove. Because if you ask me, he's been far too gentlemanly about you, honey. He needs to drag you off to his cave by the hair.'

Morgan snorted. 'Gentlemanly? You must be joking! He's . . . but go on. This is fascinating,' she said acidly.

Ryan shrugged, 'Well, I just thought that if I could make him jealous—you know, let him think I might be making out where he failed, it might just do the trick?' he finished meekly.

Morgan closed her eyes and said in a strangled voice, 'Just how did you plan to achieve that, Ryan?' not sure whether she wanted to hit him or laugh hysterically.

'Ah,' said Ryan. 'Now there's my problem. Despite my powerful brain I couldn't quite work it out. Er . . . you still with me, Morgan?'

'Oh, Ryan,' she said helplessly. 'Someone should have warned me about you. And how do you think Sheila would have appreciated that? Look,' she added, 'I appreciate your motives, I really do, but it's not the solution. And if you don't believe me, why don't you ask Sheila?'

He sat staring at her with his hands folded in his lap. Finally he said with an effort, 'Sheila mightn't thank me now, but I'm sure it's the only solution for her. And I'm prepared to wait, Morgan. Incidentally, I'm sure it's the only solution for you too. All right, all right!' He raised a hand. 'Don't say it. But you did promise to tell me something in exchange for these confidences.'

Morgan ground her teeth. 'I'm telling you nothing until you promise me that you'll drop any mad ideas you have of making Steve jealous.'

'I promise,' he said gravely. 'I realise it was a stupid idea.'

'I'm so glad to hear you say so,' she retorted sardonically. 'No, for what it's worth, I haven't passed on the good news. But I will. . . . May I help you?' she said to a prospective customer, and with an acute sense of relief plunged gratefully into a most complicated tour of all the southern, thoroughbred breeding establishments because her client, as it turned out, was a mad gambler who had been fired with enthusiasm over the Queensland Winter Racing Carnival and now cherished a burning ambition to own a galloper.

She thought briefly once, and longingly, of the simplicity of finding crocodiles by comparison, and finally, in desperation and spurred on by Ryan's barely concealed chuckles, she made a phone call to one of the Turf Clubs to beg the young gentleman on the other end, with tears in her eyes, for all the information he possessed on southern studs.

'At least their localities,' she pleaded. 'You see,' she swivelled her chair round and said confidentially into the phone, 'I'm a travel consultant and have this person who's determined to visit every stud in the Commonwealth of

Australia! And our motto is that no trip is too large or too small for us to handle. Could you help me?'

'I certainly can,' said the voice on the other end of the line. There was a slight hesitation. Then, 'Do you have a lunch hour? Because if you were to give me just a little time to gather my information, I'd be only to happy to pass it on in person. Shall we say,' he named the coffee bar of an hotel, 'in about an hour?'

Morgan coughed and glanced at the eager face of her client. 'Very well,' she said reluctantly. 'How will I know you, though?'

'I'll be wearing a red carnation in my buttonhole,' said the voice. 'See you later, Miss Jones!'

She slammed the phone down and compressed her lips. 'Now see what you've led me into,' she muttered in a fierce aside to Ryan, then switched a completely disarming smile on to her portly client and assured him that the kind of tour he required was quite within the power of her agency to arrange. Given a little time!

Morgan stared at the red carnation undeniably in the buttonhole of a superbly cut, navy-blue suit with a faint white stripe in it and pondered painfully on just how deceiving voices could be.

For this was no eager young man whom she'd pictured rather in Ryan's class. No, this was certainly no Ryan, this well-preserved man-about-town with his sophisticated manner, beautifully tended moustache and bedroom eyes.

'By George!' said the gentleman in a deep-timbred, well-bred voice as they shook hands. 'How do you do, Miss Jones?

'How do you do?' Morgan replied, and contrived to assume an air of insouciance at her companion's speculative gaze.

'Do you know,' he said, still clasping her hand, 'I've just had a much better idea. Quaint as this little coffee bar is, I'm sure we'd be much more comfortable in the restaurant proper. And I happen to know they do a superb oxtail casserole at this time of year. How does that sound to you?'

'Er ... very nice,' she said wryly, and suppressed a rueful grin as she accepted her hand back.

The restaurant was very elegant and certainly more comfortable, although it was also very well populated. It seemed a lot of people knew about the superb oxtail casserole, Morgan thought, as they were led to a small table that was obviously a late placement between two others, one of which accommodated a large noisy party which not only attracted the attention of other diners but also the press.

Morgan blinked as the flashbulbs popped and wondered idly who they were next door.

'Now,' said her companion, 'why don't you tell me all about yourself, my dear?'

Morgan was never quite sure what got into her, but that her reply was provocative she did not doubt. 'Tell me first about the studs,' she pleaded. 'My job really depends on it!'

He looked at her amusedly and cradled his wine-glass in his two hands. 'I have it all written down,' he told her, and put his glass down to reach into his pocket. 'There you are, my dear. There's a printed brochure too. It's all there,' he added reassuringly.

'Thank you,' said Morgan, and allowed her eyes to roll back expressively. 'If you knew what this means to me ...!'

The man cleared his throat and took a gulp of his wine. 'Why don't you tell me?'

Morgan pondered as she toyed with her oxtail. 'I have this boss,' she explained on an urgent note that was a credit to her unsuspected acting ability. 'He's ... well, he's a pig really.'

'Go on,' said her companion keenly.

'He keeps threatening me,' she said tragically.

'How do you mean?'

'Well,' Morgan lowered her gaze and decided that the oxtail was really delicious. 'Put it this way,' she said, hastily wrenching her mind back, 'I know if I went to bed with him, I wouldn't have to worry how I did my job. But,' she added sadly, 'because I won't, he's on my back all the time. If you could see him,' she said forlornly, and at the same time sent up a little prayer for forgiveness because in fact her boss was a small neat man totally devoted to his wife and five children. She shuddered dramatically. 'He gives me the creeps,' she said in a small but expressive voice, and swallowed another mouthful.

'Oh, my dear,' said her companion, and reached out to cover her hand with one of his own. 'My dear little girl!' he repeated as she gazed soulfully up into his eyes.

It was the bright light of a flashbulb exploding that brought Morgan to her senses. It seemed to be particularly close. But she acted theatrically still. A hand flew to her mouth as much to hide her inner laughter as anything and, galvanised into action, she took a last mouthful, rose to her feet, gathered the papers that lay neatly on the table between them and said in a choked voice, 'I must go! I've said too much. . . . Oh, how can I thank you—for the lunch as well,' and fled without a backward glance.

'So,' she said to her gambling client later that afternoon, 'there it is.'

'You've done wonders, Miss Jones,' he replied enthusiastically. 'To think,' he fingered a close-written sheet absently, 'this morning when I came in I was in a position to purchase a successor to Phar Lap or Bernborough. . . .' His eyes filled with real tears and Morgan stared at him as he smote his brow with a clenched fist.

'What is it?' she asked anxiously.

'I've blown it all. Well, almost,' he said tragically, and

withdrew a small transistor radio from his pocket. 'On the Daily Double at Royal Randwick today. It's uncanny, isn't it? I mean the first leg, which I picked, incidentally, romped away to win four lengths at *twenty* to one! But my choice in the second leg which, mind you, was the five to two favourite, ran stone motherless!'

'Do you mean you're not going on this trip?' Morgan enquired with a slight crack in her voice.

'Sadly no. Not this year, my dear. But I can't thank you enough for your trouble. And I shall certainly come back to you if the position ever changes. Er ... may I keep this information? I can pore over it and dream a little, can't I?' he said ingenuously. 'Thank you again!' he added over his shoulder as he headed for the door.

Morgan turned on Ryan. 'Don't you dare laugh!' she warned. 'If you knew what I went through to get all that stuff!'

'Oh, but I do!'

It was the next morning, Thursday in fact, and Ryan was filling in the last few minutes before the doors opened, reading the paper.

'Oh boy, do I ever?' He whistled and passed the page obligingly over to Morgan. 'Check that,' he said gleefully.

Morgan stared at the paper and then closed her eyes.

'Read it!' Ryan insisted, and clicked his tongue as he leant over her shoulder and ran his finger along the caption beneath a clear, unmistakable photograph of herself gazing soulfully into the eyes of yesterday's lunch companion.

' "Eligible bachelor and man-about-town Errol Soames captured in an intimate moment with beautiful mystery companion ... da dah, da dah, seen lunching together yesterday. Mr Soames refused to be drawn on the identity of the lovely lady, but if the gleam in his eye was anything to go by, it appears he was most taken with his glamorous companion." Refused to be drawn, eh? I wonder why?' Ryan said inquisitively, his features positively alive with sparkling curiosity.

'Possibly because he only knows me as Miss Jones,' Morgan retorted.

'But he knows where you work?'

'Yes,' she said bitterly. 'But if he sets foot inside that door I shall just get up and run out the back way and *you* can deal with him!'

'Why me?' Ryan protested with a laugh.

'Because if you hadn't been driving me mad yesterday with all your questions, I wouldn't have got myself into this. That's why!' she said fiercely.

'But why were you looking at him like that?' Ryan asked, his eyes alight with laughter.

'Mind your own business,' she said tartly.

'Have you told Harrow you're not working for him any more?'

'Now what on earth has that got to do with this, Ryan?' Her voice rose shrilly.

'Nothing,' Ryan said hastily. 'But have you?'

She took a deep breath. 'No, I haven't—not yet. But I will. And those are the last words I'm prepared to utter on the subject. Do you read me right, Ryan?' she asked with a dangerous glitter in her eyes.

'Roger willco!' Ryan said obligingly, and was as good as his word for the rest of the day, although if Morgan had been less busy she might have noticed that he looked unusually thoughtful on the odd occasion.

Morgan could hear her phone ringing as she approached her front door. She grappled with her key, but as usual, when one tries to hurry, she found her fingers fumbling and consequently by the time she got the door open she was breathless and quite convinced the phone would stop ringing just as she got there.

She snatched the receiver up. 'Hullo!'

'Oh! Hullo. I was just going to give up,' said a perfectly strange voice.

'Yes. I was outside. Who is that?' Morgan asked.

'You don't know me, Miss Jones, but I'm a friend of Steve Harrow's and it's on his behalf that I'm ringing. The thing is he's had an accident and broken his leg. . . .'

Morgan gasped. 'How? I mean when? Is he in hospital? Is he all right?'

'He's home in plaster,' said the voice. 'But as you can imagine, he's quite incapacitated and . . . and—well, he's asking for you, so I thought. . . .'

'Asking for me?' Morgan said incredulously. 'Are you sure?'

'Yes—well, it seems to be tied up with some work you're doing for him as well. Look, I was wondering, if you're not doing anything this evening, if you'd be able to come up and see him. You know how invalids are, especially when they're in pain. Would you be able to do that, Miss Jones? I'd really appreciate it.'

'I . . . I . . . well,' Morgan began disjointedly. 'I guess so,' she added. 'If you're sure?'

'Quite sure. Say—in about an hour?'

'I . . . yes,' she said dazedly, and put the phone down slowly.

Then with a bewildered sigh she hurried to change her clothes, gathered up the manuscript and typewriter and headed for her car, only stopping to collect her mail and bundle it unopened into her handbag.

And all during the long drive westwards she kept biting her lip and wincing inwardly as she pictured Steve in pain and confined to crutches. But another thought interspersed itself as she turned into his driveway and found no other car parked in beneath the deck. A tiny frown grew on her forehead. Surely he wasn't alone?

She climbed out of the car juggling the manuscript and

the typewriter and decided against knocking on the door.
Instead she tried the handle and found it unlocked. As
she climbed the stairs she could hear the throb of music
and was tempted to call out, but doubted if she could
make herself heard above Mendelssohn's Violin Concerto
in full quadraphonic sound.

So it was that she arrived at the top of the staircase
unheralded. And what she saw caused her eyes to widen
and her mouth to form a soundless O of bewilderment.

The lamps in the lounge were dimmed, but in the firelight there was no mistaking Steve Harrow's tall lithe
figure standing on the edge of the oyster beige carpet with
his back to her as he stared out over the lights of the
greater Brisbane area. Something in his hand caught the
light and she realised it was a crystal glass half full of
amber liquid which he raised to his mouth and drained,
and then with a powerful arc of his arm, he flung the
glass outwards and over the deck railing in a violent gesture of disgust that made Morgan gasp and even imagine
she could hear the crystal shattering on the rocks below.

He swung round abruptly and his eyes fell on her and
narrowed as if in disbelief.

She tried to speak, but it was as if her vocal chords had
gone on strike, and it was he who broke the silence as the
last sweet note of music trembled on the air and floated
away.

'What the devil are you doing here?' he demanded
harshly.

She swallowed and heard the record player click off.
'You're ... not in plaster?' she whispered as her bewildered eyes travelled slowly up and down his navy-blue
shirt unbuttoned almost to the waist, and his well-fitting
pale-grey cord trousers.

He frowned. 'Did you say in plaster? Why should I be
in plaster?'

'But someone rang me up. A friend of yours. He said

. . . you were asking for me. . . .' Her voice trailed off helplessly. She lowered the typewriter slowly to the floor because her legs no longer felt quite steady.

'I was asking for you?' Steve echoed with a wealth of sardonic amusement. 'Why the hell should I do that?' he asked coldly.

Morgan raised her free hand to her brow and wondered if she was imagining all this. But another look at his grim, set face assured her she was not imagining him at least.

'Look,' she said with all the calm she could muster, 'about an hour ago someone rang me up at home, and said you'd had an accident and broken your leg . . . said you were home in plaster and . . . and wanted to see me about your book!' Her voice rose at the look of scornful disbelief. 'I tell you they did!' she insisted angrily.

'So you came running like some ministering angel?' he retorted, and with a sudden movement flung himself down in one of the armchairs. 'I don't pretend to know what's going on, Morgan,' he said, staring across at her with eyes colder than she'd ever seen them, 'but as you see, I don't have any broken limbs. You sure your neuroses haven't taken over entirely?' he enquired with a derisive quirk to his lips that made her squirm inwardly.

'Well, I hate to disappoint you,' she said tightly, 'but unless *you* can come up with a better explanation *I'm* going to think you deliberately lured me up here!' She stamped her foot angrily.

'Now, I hate to sound like a broken record, my dear Morgan, but just exactly why the hell would I want to do that?' He looked her up and down disparagingly from beneath half-closed lids. 'I might add—unless *you* come up with a better explanation I could be tempted to think something similar. Did you have a rush of blood perhaps and decide my first lesson in loving was so successful you'd come for another?'

She followed his eyes as they flicked across the room to

where the morning papers lay scattered carelessly on the floor and knew her face paled as her eyes widened. Because even from this distance she had no difficulty in distinguishing the social page lying uppermost.

She licked her lips and started to speak, but quite incoherently even to herself until he stood up impatiently and strode across the room to tower over her menacingly.

'Well, let me tell you, Miss Jones,' he said caustically through gritted teeth, 'you're doing just fine on your own, sweetheart. Despite a slow start you've learnt—oh, so quickly! I'm sure I'd only be superfluous. Or perhaps you've come here to taunt me? Is that it?' He laughed unpleasantly. 'You're wasting your time, Glamorgan.'

She took a step backwards and put out a hand as if to ward off his words that seemed to be striking her like blows. And then the beautiful lamplight room began to swirl around her and she staggered and would have fallen if he hadn't reached for her. But not quickly enough to prevent the manuscript from slipping from her fingers to scatter loosely at her feet.

The last thing she was conscious of as he swung her into his arms was the single sharp expletive he uttered as if goaded beyond endurance.

CHAPTER TEN

SHE came to to find herself propped up in the corner of the settee. Steve was holding a glass to her lips. 'Take a sip,' he said quietly as her eyes fluttered open.

She did, and coughed as the fiery liquid slipped down her throat. He put the glass down and picked up one of her hands to massage it. 'You fainted,' he said. 'Why?'

'I didn't. . . .'

'No, Morgan,' he interrupted, 'don't tell me you didn't have enough to eat at lunch.'

'Well, I didn't, as a matter of fact,' she said wanly, 'but. . . .' She sat upright with a jerk. 'Oh no!' she exclaimed with her hand to her lips.

'What is it?'

'Are you quite sure. . . ?' she began agitatedly.

'Yes, I'm quite sure I haven't broken my leg,' he interjected wryly. 'I think I would have known.'

'I mean . . . I can see that, but. . . .' She broke off abruptly. Then she said almost questioningly, 'Ryan? Would he? Oh no! Surely Ryan wouldn't have done it, would he?' she asked again as if begging for reassurance.

Steve raised his eyebrows quizzically and presented the glass to her lips. 'Have another sip,' he advised.

She pushed his hand away sharply. 'I'm all right now, really. But I don't understand how I came to be here tonight! I . . . in fact I'd sworn I'd never willingly lay eyes on you again,' she said tearfully. 'I was going to send your precious manuscript back by mail. And that's another thing! I can see where your book is leading now. Do you know,' she went on, her voice thickened with emotion,

'I admired Leonie above all the others. But you . . . *that's* going to be the twist in the tail, isn't it? She's the murderer . . . murderess, isn't she? But why?'

He was silent for a moment, his eyes narrowed and enigmatic as he looked at her. Then he said dryly, 'You'll have to read the next instalment, Morgan. Why does Leonie appeal to you so much?'

'I don't know,' she said brokenly after a moment. 'Perhaps because she's everything I knew I could never be. Someone who could love without counting the cost. Love your hero so much that when she discovered he was pinching the secrets and not the other way round she'd . . . she'd even resort to murder to protect him,' she said with a slight catch in her voice.

Steve stood up. 'You've pre-empted me slightly, Morgan. If she loved him so much, why isn't she standing up to take the rap for him? But apart from that, don't you think people *can* be driven to those kind of excesses out of their feelings for someone?'

'Do *you*? Really, I mean?' she countered painfully as she looked up at him with wide, still tear-filled eyes.

He stared down at her broodingly for a long moment, then he shrugged. 'Do I? I'm not quite sure. Er . . . to get back to reality, though, you mentioned your mate Ryan Clarke before we got sidetracked. What has he got to do with all this?' he asked.

Morgan sat forward and wrested the glass from his grasp to take a long swallow. What indeed? she asked herself. If you but knew!

'Well,' she said, spluttering slightly, 'you don't have a broken leg—yet as sure as I'm sitting here, I swear I got that phone call! I . . . just can't think who else it could have been,' she added tentatively.

'I'm afraid I'm still not with you,' he said as he moved away to pour himself a drink. 'Is Ryan a practical joker extraordinaire?'

'N-not really,' she said, and bit her lip as she begun to wish heartily that she'd never mentioned Ryan's name.

Steve came back and sat down beside her on the broad settee. He looked at with his brows raised again. 'He's not,' he said patiently as if he was humouring a child. 'I see.' He chewed a knuckle thoughtfully. 'But he saw fit to bring you up here tonight on a wild goose chase—you reckon anyway. Why would he do that?' he glanced at her ironically.

'Because . . . because he thinks—well, the way you do,' she finished bitterly. 'Or did at least. . . .' She stopped short. What am I to say? she asked herself. Oh, Ryan, if only I had my hands round your neck this minute! You must have set this up somehow. And that has to be why you kept asking me if. . . .

She turned her head away and took another sip of her drink because Steve was now looking patently amused. 'I have to laugh at that,' he said politely, and put out a restraining hand. 'I wouldn't take it too quickly,' he advised, and looked at her glass pointedly. 'Not on an empty stomach.'

'Do you mean you don't believe me? That he did it?' she asked.

'To be honest, my dear Morgan, I'm as confused as hell—as much about Ryan's motive as the rest of it. For starters, there must have been someone else in on it or you'd have recognised his voice, wouldn't you? And another thing—how would he have known I'd be here this evening? I wonder. . . .' he added dryly, and stood up to stride across to the phone.

'Wonder what?' she asked anxiously.

He opened the telephone book and drew his finger down the first page. He said absently, 'I got this call earlier from someone who claimed they were speaking from the international telephone exchange. Er . . . to advise me that a person-to-person call had been booked through to me from overseas at eight o'clock. I didn't recognise the name they gave, but I told them to put it through anyway because I'd be home all evening.'

He dialled a number and stood leaning against the wall as he made his enquiry. 'I see. You're quite sure?' he said finally after several delays. 'No. No, don't bother. Thank you very much.' He put the phone down and swung round to face Morgan.

'That call was a hoax,' he said quietly. 'A rather ingenious way of making sure I'd be here. Morgan,' he strolled over to her and looked down at her searchingly, 'I'm going to make us something to eat. And in the meantime you might like to try and sort out your friend Ryan's motives, because I'm most interested,' he added with a sudden glint in his eye that told her she was going to have a hard time squirming out of this one. 'No.' He put out a hand as she moved restlessly. 'You relax here by the fire while I do it,' he said with a note of command in his voice.

Morgan did as she was bid. For two reasons—for the moment she felt too weary and drained to do anything else. And secondly, something about him told her that he'd have no qualms about stopping her, if she tried to leave.

She stared into the flames and thought back over the incredible events of the evening. Of how hard and angry he had been when she had first arrived. Even before he knew she was there, she realised, and shivered as she recalled the glass he'd deliberately smashed, curving through the firelit air.

But that couldn't have been to do with me, she mused. Maybe ... she sat up suddenly. Maybe it was Sheila? Oh no, she thought a little wildly. Could *that* crazy plan of Ryan's have worked in reverse? she wondered. Could it be that Sheila was using Ryan to make Steve jealous?

She took a sip from her drink and rubbed her finger round the rim of her glass. Is he having second thoughts? she mused. Perhaps he regrets giving Sheila her marching orders now. Oh dear!

Sounds from the kitchen penetrated her mind and she tried to gather her wits hastily. What was she to tell him about Ryan? The truth—that he'd fallen head over heals in love with Sheila? And more—or rather worse—that he thought she was being stupid and stubborn about . . . but how could she say it? Look, Steve, she mimicked herself in her mind, Ryan's quite convinced I'm madly in love with you, and that's why he decided to force us to get together.

And she pictured his reply quite clearly and winced as the object of her thoughts arrived silently on the scene pushing a small chrome trolley on well oiled wheels. She started and coloured, and to hide her discomfort, stared at the appetising meal for two set out on it. There were steaming bowls of soup and some crisp rolls nestling in a white linen napkin, also a larger dish standing above a little blue flame and emitting a tantalising smell.

She sniffed appreciatively before she could stop herself.

Steve handed her a napkin and drew up a chair for himself. 'Homemade mushroom soup and chicken in wine. How does that sound?'

'Delicious,' she said quietly. 'You have so many talents, I'm amazed sometimes.' She peeped at him from beneath her lashes to see how he took this attempt to normalise a peculiar situation.

'Thank you,' he said politely. 'I'm reliably informed you're no mean hand with the wooden spoon yourself.'

She grimaced. 'If you're referring to Brad, he has the most enormous appetite, but I don't think he's exactly a gourmet.'

He grinned slightly. 'You're right about his appetite. I

was afraid I was going to have to offer him some witchety grubs—or come back early from the trip because he'd eaten us bare. How is he, by the way?'

'Pretty good. I . . . I haven't had much time this week to spend with him, but I promised him. . . .' Her voice trailed away. She began again. 'What I mean. . . .'

'What you mean is you promised to spend more time tutoring him once you'd washed your hands of my manuscript . . . and me?' asked Steve on an ironic note.

'I didn't wash my hands of it,' she said steadily. 'I got it up to date for you and in precise money terms—if you must know, I've repaid my debt and a bit over.' She glanced around to see that all her hard work had been gathered up carelessly and now lay on the dining room table.

'I did think, however,' he said as he dished up the chicken, 'that we had an agreement to work together until it was finished. Yet you *did* mention earlier that you'd decided never to see me again. I wonder why? Because of what transpired the last time we met? Maybe because you were so disappointed in my treatment of Leonie? Or . . .?'

'Don't you think I had any right to be upset about . . . about our last meeting?' she asked jerkily.

He shrugged and allowed his eyes to flicker over her impersonally. 'If the cap fits, wear it,' he said with a return of the underlying roughness in his voice. 'Talking of hats—or rather clothes,' he went on, unperturbed by her flashing look, 'shouldn't you take your jacket off? You'll need it later when you go home.'

Morgan sat with her knife and fork poised as she tried to adjust her mind to this mundane topic. Then she looked down at the green velvet blazer she wore over a fine cream Vyella blouse and a beautifully tailored matching cream suede skirt.

'I suppose I should,' she agreed, and stood up to do it. In the process she accidentally brushed off one of her gold-link hoop ear-rings. She bent to retrieve it from the carpet, but Steve was before her and she felt strangely transfixed as she knelt on the carpet with her gleaming hair falling in her face, staring at the strands of gold lying in his hand like a delicate teardrop.

He had leant over the arm of his chair to pick it up and he straightened slowly to inspect the ear-ring more closely with his eyes narrowed.

Morgan looped her hair back nervously and put out her hand for it.

'Is it new?' he asked as he fingered it.

'No. Why do you ask?'

'I've never noticed you wearing them before, that's all,' he said absently, and handed it back to her as he switched his gaze to his meal.

She stood up and swung her head so that her hair flew out in an arc revealing her ear-lobe.

'No,' she said again as she screwed it into place. 'It's a relic from my more affluent days. But they have this habit of falling off for the least reason. That's why I don't wear them often.'

She sat down and picked up her knife and fork, but between mouthfuls she found herself studying his face as unobtrusively as she could. Because, she realised, something about him frightened her this evening. But it wasn't the usual fear she had when she was with him—that by some gesture she couldn't prevent making her treacherous desires known to him.

No, she thought, this is different. Deep down he's coldly yet violently angry. She shivered slightly and started as his gold-tipped lashes lifted suddenly and his eyes met hers. She looked down immediately but couldn't prevent a faint flush from rising to her cheeks.

Steve said as he pushed his plate away, 'Tell me about

Ryan now.' He reached for the coffee pot and poured himself a cup.

Morgan put her knife and fork down precisely. 'It was good,' she said. 'Very good.'

'Morgan,' he said quietly, 'we've been through all this before. The first time you had dinner here you were most complimentary. I'll take it as read now, so don't try and use it to sidetrack me. Do you think it would help you to loosen your tongue—about Mr Ryan Clarke anyway—if I poured you a liqueur? Because I intend to get to the bottom of this come hell or high water. I don't particularly appreciate being the object of this kind of joke or whatever it is.'

She accepted the glass of liqueur with a fleeting upward glance and fought a sincere desire to get up and run from him, he looked so cold and grim. She licked her lips and waited for him to sit down before she said, 'Ryan is . . . I think he's very fond of me. Rather like a brother,' she added, and clenched her fingers around the stem of her glass at the cynical look he cast her. 'It's true,' she said quietly. If only I could tell you about Sheila, you'd realise just how true it was, she thought. 'And I'm very fond of him,' she added hastily. Which is also true, she thought. Nine times out of ten, that is. 'Anyway,' she forced herself to go on, 'he. . . .' She sought for the right words, but instead sighed suddenly and shrugged helplessly.

'Oh, look,' she said on a sharper note, 'if you must know, he agrees entirely with you about me. He thinks I'm headed for a life of self-imposed spinsterhood and he thinks I'm crazy. As if it's any of his business—or yours, for that matter!' She flashed him another angry look and took a sip of her drink.

'Go on,' he said impassively.

'There's not much more to say,' she retorted.

'You mean that by some form of extra-sensory perception, he divined what was going on between us and out of his brotherly love for you decided to set us up?' he offered sombrely. 'Is that what you're trying to tell me?'

'Yes,' she said bleakly.

'Well, I find it hard to believe, Morgan. Is he a mind-reader? And is there a man alive who could be so altruistic towards a gorgeous girl like you? You did tell me yourself he tried to "dally" with you at least once a day, didn't you? I wonder if he couldn't have had some other motive?'

Oh, he did indeed, Morgan thought. Only I'm not game to tell you what it is!

'What other motive could he have had?' she asked as she stood up restlessly, totally unsure of how to deal with this situation.

He didn't say anything as she wandered across to the dining-room table. But when she turned back to him it was to see him contemplating his glass with that same look of cynicism.

'Do you believe a word I've said?' she queried sardonically, thinking at the same time that it *was* true—just not the whole truth.

'I'll tell you later,' Steve commented dryly as he swirled the liquid in his glass and raised it to his lips. 'But you haven't answered my other question. Is Ryan a mind-reader?'

'Well, not exactly,' she said, and felt a faint sense of relief at having moved to slightly less dangerous ground. 'In fact,' she added shortly, 'if you must know, the Spanish Inquisition could have only benefited with the addition of Ryan on their team. He's curious to a fault and he has this way of pinning you down and making you squirm!' Which was also true, she muttered, but beneath her breath.

'Does he indeed?' He reached for his coffee cup.

She wandered back across the room and sat down

uneasily on the edge of the settee.

Steve frowned down at the dregs in his cup. 'I don't understand one thing,' he said lazily. 'What would you have to squirm about?'

The question seemed to echo oddly.

'I mean,' he went on smoothly, 'you're so sure you're right about yourself—in relation to me anyway, aren't you? How can he make you squirm, then?'

She didn't reply, mainly because her tongue seemed to have tied itself in knots.

'Aren't you, Morgan?' he said again with dangerous quiet.

'Yes,' she said miserably at last. Then she cried, 'But like you ... at least, like you were, he won't accept it! Which is really an impertinence. I. . . .'

'I gather he knew you'd sworn never to see me again?' he asked coolly, overriding her agitation imperturbably and making her feel like a troublesome fly.

She gritted her teeth. 'Yes, he did,' she said tartly.

'Well then,' he shrugged, and stood up. 'Maybe he's not aware of this,' he said casually over his shoulder as he strolled over to where the paper lay on the floor. 'Why don't you show it to him, Morgan, and tell him he's flogging a dead horse as far as I'm concerned but there's no need to give up hope on your account. In fact you're coming along beautifully.' He let the social page flutter into her lap. 'I presume you've seen it?' he added.

Morgan took a deep breath and threw the paper away from her. 'What a good idea,' she said. 'I'll do just that!' She managed to speak calmly, although inside she was a seething mass of rage.

She stood up and gathered her blazer in one hand. 'Now that it's all sorted out, I think I'll take my leave. I do apologise for my friend Ryan. And I can guarantee it won't happen again,' she added lightly, and made to move past him as he stood in the middle of the room regarding her thoughtfully.

But he put out a hand languidly and caught her arm. 'Yes, do that, Morgan,' he said gently, and then with a swift movement that took her by surprise and caused her to drop her handbag and blazer, he pulled her into his arms in a bruising embrace and tilted her head backwards with rough fingers beneath her chin so that she was forced to stare into his eyes.

'What are you . . . doing?' she stammered. 'Let me go!'

'Not just yet, Morgan,' he said softly but with each word cutting and measured. 'Not until you tell me what really made you change. What it is about this man that attracts, sweetheart? Academically I find it very interesting. Also, I'm prepared to manhandle you like this—until you tell me the truth!'

'Like this' was to lower his head to claim her lips in a brutal punishing kiss that seemed to last for ever, while at the same time his hard fingers moved around her shoulders and then down the slender sweep of her back to her waist, leaving a trail of bruises.

Then when she felt she could no longer breathe, he raised his head suddenly and, swearing coldly, almost flung her away from him so that she collapsed on to the settee and turned away from her to shove his hands into his pockets and stare into the fire.

Morgan stayed where she was, too exhausted and breathless to move and with silent tears streaming down her cheeks. Until he turned back to her and picked up her handbag and dropped it in her lap. 'You better do whatever it is women do to themselves when they need to pull themselves together,' he ground out as he towered over her. 'Because you're leaving very shortly, Morgan, you. . . .'

She shrank back into the settee, her eyes now wide and fearful at the menace in his voice.

'Go on,' he said contemptuously. 'Get all your war-paint out. You've got two minutes. I'm not going to lay a finger on you, so you don't have to look so stricken.'

She swallowed convulsively and fumbled with the catch of her handbag. As it happened she had no 'warpaint' with her, but she pulled a hanky out and closed her eyes in exasperation as her unopened mail spilled out and slippped off her lap to the floor. She gathered the small pile together with jerky fingers, but one evaded her. She reached for it and with her fingers on it, hesitated and stared. It was a black-bordered envelope with an overseas postmark. A Welsh postmark. . . .

She lifted it with a sudden cry of anguish and jumped to her feet, scattering everything else again as she did but uncaring and unaware and intent only on this one letter.

She wrested if from its envelope with fingers that trembled anew and started to read.

'No . . . oh no! It's not true!' she sobbed as the lines wavered and blurred before her eyes. Then with the letter pressed to her she swung round suddenly and ran across the room, down the staircase and out into the dark cold night, sobbing desperately.

CHAPTER ELEVEN

MORGAN lay on a bed of spiky grass, her breath coming as if it was wrenched from her lungs, then she sat up cautiously and felt her ankle. In her headlong rush down the rough hillside she'd tripped over a rock—fortunately a large smooth rock that was raised barely an inch above the ground, but it had been enough to send her sprawling.

She pushed herself off the ground with her hands and tested the ankle, sighing with relief when it bore her weight. She stood upright, panting with exertion so that her breath hung in the chill night air. Then she felt the crackle of paper beneath her fingers and realised she still held the letter in one hand. Realised anew why she was out on the hillside and what had motivated her to run away like that as if she could run away from life itself, and she gave a low despairing moan. She wrapped her arms around the tree trunk and laid her cheek against its smooth white bark, sobbing desolately.

'I should have gone. I *knew* I should have gone!'

She jumped as a hand touched her shoulder and turned to see Steve Harrow behind her in the moonlight.

'Morgan. . . .'

'Get away from me!' she snapped. 'Do you hear me!' Her voice rose hysterically and her teeth chattered with cold.

But he stood there looking down at her, impassively she thought, and this on top of everything else so incensed her that she turned on him like some wild creature, flailing at him with her fists. Still he stood there, accepting the rain of puny blows until she thought she'd die of frustration.

Then he made a move to pick her up in his arms, although she resisted until he said coolly, 'I'll knock you out if you don't come quietly, Morgan,' and gathered her up as if she was a child in a grasp that smothered any chance of further resistance and with such powerful ease, it made a mockery of her previous efforts and she went limp in his arms.

Oh dear, was her last coherent thought for a little while as Steve mounted the spiral staircase as if he was only carrying a bundle of kindling, I'm mad! I'm quite crazy! I suppose he'll start accusing me of being more neurotic than ever. Oh dear. . . .

'Oh no!' however, was what she said aloud as he carried her through the lounge room to his bedroom and deposited her on the bed on top of the ruby velvet spread. 'Oh no!'

'Oh yes, Morgan,' he said flatly, and bent to remove her shoes. 'Now,' he straightened and added impersonally, 'can you lift yourself? I want to take the cover off.' He didn't give her much chance to react before sweeping the cover and blankets and top sheet aside beneath her. 'There,' he said as she floundered helplessly, 'stay still now, I'll cover you up.' And so saying he swept the covers back over her. 'I'll fix the fire. You stay where you are.'

Morgan lay there obediently. Not because he told me to, she told herself wearily, but because I don't know where to go, and besides, I just don't have the strength. Oh, Morgan!

But her eyes widened at the strange sound she heard of wood squeaking on wood and she tilted her head enquiringly as Steve came back into the bedroom bearing two steaming cups which he placed beside her.

'I've never tried this before,' he said conversationally as he touched the wooden wall opposite the bed.

Morgan gasped as a section folded neatly against its adjacent companion rather like a telephone booth door to reveal the grate and fireplace.

'How did you do that!' she asked, momentarily diverted.

'It's a two-way fireplace,' he replied, and came to sit on the side of the bed. 'You can shut it off from the other side. Here,' he handed her a cup.

'Wh—what is it?' she stammered.

'Laced coffee. I think you've had enough straight medicinal alcohol. I gather from your agitation and the envelope you left on the floor that your father's died, Morgan?'

She closed her eyes and felt him remove the cup from her grasp as the tears trickled down her cheeks. 'Yes,' she said desolately.

'Why didn't they telegraph you?'

'Read the letter,' she said tonelessly.

He bent to pick the crumpled sheet from the floor where she had finally dropped it.

' "... inform you your father, God rest his soul, departed this temporal life unexpectedly, dear niece. You will be wondering why I didn't inform you of this more urgently, but it was his last expressed wish when he realised the Lord was indeed to claim him, Glamorgan. In fact his last words were—I love her, but my greatest sin was never to let her know. Bury me fast, then let her know. And if the weight of my love has been too great on her, Lord forgive me. For she was the only offspring I knew and the most precious".'

'I had this feeling,' she said as his deep voice trailed away. 'Increasingly I had this feeling ... that he really cared, but couldn't express it somehow. Then when he was taken ill and his brother wrote to me I just sent the money over so that he could have the best of everything. But all along—deep down—I knew it wasn't the National Health he was objecting to but that somehow he felt he wasn't going to weather this storm and was pleading with me to go to him. But I ignored what my heart told me. Oh God!' She dropped her head into her hands so that the tears trickled through her fingers.

'Morgan,' said Steve gently with a sudden look of comprehension, 'at least you did that. It's no small thing to part with your life's savings. I only wish you'd told me.'

'It's too late!' She raised her tear-stained face to him. 'There's nothing you can say that will make it any different. And I did try to tell you—well, I thought of it anyway.' She dropped her head disconsolately.

'Glamorgan, look at me,' he said deliberately, and captured one of her hands. 'I'm sorry about your father, but. . . .'

'So you should be,' she said irrationally, 'because if you can't understand me, how do you think I felt all my life? I never understood him until it was too late!'

'All right,' he said steadily, 'but you've worked it out and you mustn't upset yourself like this.'

She pushed his hand away. 'Why shouldn't I? Isn't that what you and Ryan are telling me constantly? To *feel*? Well, I'm feeling now, if it's any consolation to you. I've never felt worse. I ran out on a sick dying man who was my father.' She stared down at the velvet beneath her hand.

'Look,' he said at last, 'seeing you're already in bed why don't you try to sleep? A good sleep often works wonders,' he added wryly, and reached across her to pull more pillows beneath her head. 'It's warm in here and I'll only be next door and we can talk again tomorrow. Lie back, Morgan.'

She hesitated and then slowly allowed herself to relax against the pillows as he moved around the room and then across to the door to switch off the overhead light, leaving the room bathed only in the firelight.

But this brought Morgan up with a jerk. 'No!' she gasped, and scrambled out of the bed. 'No, no! I can't stay here by myself. . . .'

She stumbled across the room and tried to push past him, but he caught her in his arms with an impatient exclamation.

'Don't be an idiot,' he said roughly. 'Do you think I'd take advantage of you in this condition?' He shook her slightly and she caught a flash of blue fire in his eyes.

'It . . . it's not you,' she stammered. 'It's the Min Min. Oh, I know it's stupid, but that painting of yours makes me. . . . I just can't stay in here on my own!'

She felt him go quite still before he gathered her more closely and muttered bewilderedly over her head, 'You crazy kid! Have you ever seen the Min Min lights?'

'No, I haven't,' she said unevenly and with a still pounding heart. 'But I went on a bush holiday once up that way and your painting makes me feel as if I'm right there. I . . . the last time I slept here I didn't put the light out.'

His arms tightened about her and she surprised herself by snuggling closer involuntarily.

What am I doing? she wondered dazedly as she felt the muscles of his shoulder ripple beneath her cheek. Then— I can't help myself, but this is the only place I feel safe. And one of her hands crept up to slip beneath his shirt and lie lightly and then spread his skin with a touch as soft as silk.

'. . . . Morgan,' he said with an effort, 'do you know what you're doing?'

'Yes,' she whispered wonderingly. 'Something I should have done long ago. You were right—or was it Ryan? I can't remember any more, but there *is* only one way to get you out of my system.' She moved her head away to look up into his eyes. 'Don't worry, there'll be no recriminations,' she said huskily. 'Tomorrow I'll go away without a fuss but knowing at least . . . that I wasn't a coward.'

His eyes searched her face, but to her they were as enigmatic as ever, and when he spoke finally, his voice was as husky as hers. 'That's a very tempting offer. But what would your new boy-friend think of it?'

'Don't worry about him,' she said barely audibly. 'He'll keep.' She slid both arms around his waist.

Steve sucked in a breath and his arms tightened cruelly for a moment. Then he relaxed and murmured dryly, 'Morgan, you ought to think. . . .'

But she cut him off with a finger to his lips. 'I have thought.'

Still he delayed as their gazes locked, his eyes narrowed and intent, hers a little dreamy and tinged with wonder as she looked at him for the first time with her heart in her eyes.

'Perhaps this will convince you,' she whispered, at the same time marvelling at how easy it was. She stood on tiptoe and rested her lips provocatively on his.

'Morgan,' he said against her mouth, 'I didn't want it to be like this. But if you still feel this way when you've got over your father's death, then. . . .'

He let the sentence hang in the air and moved slightly so that it was their foreheads touching and his hands came up to circle the base of her throat. 'Think again, Morgan,' he said very quietly.

But the feel of his hands on her neck was like a burning brand even through her blouse, goading her on so that she didn't even have to think, because what she did next seemed to be the only thing she was capable of doing.

She moved within his arms and he immediately let them drop to his sides. She stepped back and with demurely downcast eyes began delicately to unbutton her blouse. And when the last button was undone she looped her hair back behind her ears with her forefingers, a graceful gesture that was peculiarly her own, and lifted her eyes to his with a look that was straight and steady.

A muscle moved in his jaw, but he didn't move.

Morgan lifted her shoulders in a tiny shrug and removed her blouse and skirt with precise and unhurried motions until she stood before him clad only in her white, lacy slip. Then she glanced up at him from beneath her lashes to see his mouth compressed in a rigid line and a trickle of apprehension ran through her because he looked so tall and strong. And forbidding.

But her mind and body were irrevocably locked into the course she'd set, and with one finger she slipped the narrow satin strap from her shoulder and reached forward to lift his hand to rest it on the pearly swelling breast she had exposed.

It seemed as if they stood etched against the firelight for a small eternity, and then the fingers of Steve's hand which had rested impassively on her breast moved to cup it and her own hand fell away as he said indistinctly this time, 'So be it. . . .' and swept her back into his embrace with one hand entwined in her hair and the other clamped hard to the small of her back so that she was moulded to him by every intimate yielding outline of her body to be kissed as he'd never kissed her before, with a passion that was strong and gentle at the same time, with a devouring intensity that she welcomed ecstatically and responded to as she'd never thought it was possible for her.

And when she finally lay on the fine cotton sheets of his bed beneath his expert hands it was as if someone else had entered her skin, her body. Someone with no fears, no inhibitions, only a driving need to please above all else.

'Morgan,' he murmured against her throat as she arched her body beneath his, 'dear God! This will hurt, and the last thing I want to do is hurt you. . . .'

But she didn't reply in the spoken word. Instead she trailed her fingers down his spine, knowing that the thought of all the pain the world could not drug her sensuous responses now. That she wanted him, needed him urgently, but above all the need to make it a worthwhile joyous experience for him stood paramount.

And she didn't flinch when the breath got caught in her throat and all she wanted to do was cry out and beg him for mercy. And she didn't allow the tears to bead her lashes until his rhythmic thrusting movements had subsided and they lay side by side both, exhausted momentarily, until he gathered her into his arms and with a gentle delicacy she would not have believed possible several minutes earlier stroked her and soothed her until unwittingly she fell asleep. And didn't know that he kissed the tears from her cheeks as he murmured her name over and over again.

It was the kookaburras that brought her awake from a dreamless sleep as they had done on the previous occasion she had slept in this bed. But as she heard their raucous calls she was for a moment completely disorientated. And then the events of the previous night washed over her and she stretched her limbs luxuriously, but only to be reclaimed by the most vivid recollections that made her turn her face to the pillow and bit her lip as her nails dug into the palms of her clenched fists.

And that she was alone in the bed seemed to confirm her worst fears. But I asked for it, she thought desolately. And I gave some promises in return. All I have to do is . . . retreat from this false position as gracefully as I can.

All? an inner voice enquired. Isn't that like trying to deny your very existence?

'Yes,' she admitted tonelessly out aloud. 'Yes. You see,' she said to herself, '*I* was right after all. Not Ryan, not Steve himself. I always knew it would be like this. Me alone . . . only it's so much worse now. . . .'

She showered and dressed like an automaton, all the time expecting to be interrupted, hoping against hope.

But no interruption came and she heard no sound to indicate any sign of life elsewhere in the house. Even the kookaburras seemed to give up, as if they'd woken too early and were slightly ashamed.

In fact she had almost convinced herself she was alone as she walked hesitantly into the lounge—and stopped short. For Steve was sitting there, sprawled in one of the blue armchairs with his hair more awry than ever and clad in the same clothes he had worn the night before but as if he'd thrown them on.

'Oh!' she breathed deeply, and closed her eyes briefly in a hopeless bid to stem the tide of vivid colour that rose from the base of her throat to her cheeks.

He didn't speak but let his eyes travel meditatively from the top of her smooth head to the tips of her toes, almost as if he was trying to memorise every detail of her appearance. Then he stood up in one lithe movement and said casually, 'Shall we have some breakfast?'

'I . . . no, thank you,' she said, finding it curiously difficult to string her words together. She looked around for her handbag and blazer and spied them on the glass dining table. 'I have to get home and get ready for work,' she added hurriedly over her shoulder. 'But thank you. . . .' She swallowed and licked her lips. *How can I say thank you?*

She jumped as she heard his voice right behind her.

'Thank you for what, Morgan?' he queried on a deceptively gentle note. 'Thank you for an offer of breakfast, thank you for dinner last night, or thank you for a one-night stand?'

She tensed as his voice roughened and he swung her round to face him with hard fingers dug into her shoulders. 'Is that all it meant to you?' he said through clenched teeth. 'The equivalent of a meal?'

'No. . . .' she said slowly, her eyes raised bravely to his. 'No. But I made a promise last night. . . .' Her voice trailed away at the blaze of anger in his eyes.

'You did a lot of things last night, Morgan,' he said curtly. 'And I can remind you of each and every one of them if you like,' he smiled coldly as she trembled beneath his hands. 'In intimate detail,' he added softly but with menace. 'Would you like me to start with the way you. . . .'

'No!' She wrenched herself away.

'But why not?' he went on silkily, and linked his fingers loosely around her wrist. 'Are you ashamed of the talent you showed last night? Does it upset you to know that you're wild and wonderful in bed? Or was it just a pre-liminary—a bid to rehearse your act and get it all together for your middle-aged Lothario?' He gestured contemptuously with his head to where the paper still lay on the floor.

Morgan stared up at him, her face paper-white and a roaring sound in her ears. 'He is not *my* middle-aged Lothario,' she said precisely. 'I met him once, and because between the two of you—you and Ryan—I was feeling goaded beyond all reason, I acted a little foolishly. Mind you, it was all in a good cause. I needed some information for a client and I got it! But I sincerely hope to God I never lay eyes on him again. He doesn't even know my first name! So put that in your pipe and smoke it,' she finished contemptuously, and tried to turn away from him.

But he wouldn't allow her to, although the only con-straint he placed on her was his hand still about her wrist. And yet that hand was as effective as a heavy chain. And it was with a flushed face and accelerated rate of breathing and bright angry eyes that she finally stood still facing him defiantly.

'All right!' she said through her teeth. 'I know you're stronger than I am. I always have! You don't have to keep proving it.'

'Is that what you think I'm doing?' he said sardonically. 'If I was intent on proving that, I'd have done it long ago, Morgan. After all, who seduced whom last night?'

But he only raised his eyebrows ironically in a way that made her squirm inwardly.

Then he released her wrist abruptly and said casually, 'I wasn't trying to prove anything, Morgan. Merely make sure that you didn't dash out in the middle of this conversation as you have a habit of doing.'

'Well, I'm not exactly,' she said coolly. 'Nor am I going to throw myself down the stairs. But I have to go—to work!' she added, her voice rising a notch. 'Surely you must realise that?'

Steve folded his arms across his chest and shrugged slightly. 'Before you go, then, Glamorgan, in view of what we shared last night, I'd like to say just one thing. I'm quite sure it won't influence you one way or another, but nonetheless I have this compulsion to say it,' he finished wryly.

'What is it?' she whispered, and thought, oh God! Is he going to tell me that he now realises what he's lost in Sheila? Because I don't think I could bear to think of them together . . . so soon. She blinked as she looked down.

'Look at me, Morgan,' he said coldly. And when she did finally, he spoke dispassionately. 'I've never slept with Sheila nor wanted to. Nor did I ever lead her to believe otherwise. What you witnessed that morning was purely circumstantial evidence. She spent the night here in much the circumstances as you did that first time. The only difference was, she brought her own gear and came with slightly different . . . expectations. Which, I admit, made it all look pretty damning. But in fact I spent the night most chastely on the settee. You see, Sheila doesn't love me.'

'But . . . but. . . .' Morgan stammered. 'I mean, the way

she looked at you, and—well, other things. It was so obvious!'

'I know,' he said bleakly. 'Yet it was deceptive too. You see, Sheila was engaged to the best friend I ever had. And when he was senselessly killed in a car accident it was . . . in a way, it was as if the light had gone out of both of our lives for a time, and quite natural that we should turn to each other. Unfortunately, as the months passed, Sheila began to transfer her feelings for Greg to me, but not to realise it for what it was—an attempt to hold on to Greg through me. If I'd never met you again, Morgan, I'd have had to break the tie sooner or later—for her sake.'

'I . . . see,' Morgan whispered. 'I'm so sorry, I didn't realise.' Oh, Ryan, she thought, you *must* be a mind-reader!

'No,' he said breaking in on her anguished thoughts, 'you wouldn't, because you deliberately refused me a chance to explain.'

She trembled at the pain of his words and dropped her eyes. It was true. But then that's the kind of person I am, she thought despairingly, and turned away this time un-hindered.

'I'll go now,' she said in a hoarse voice, and picked up her handbag and blazer. She tried to speak again, but it was impossible, and she stumbled down the stairs knowing full well that she would never be able to erase the image of Steve standing there in the lounge, unmoving, as she crept away.

But as she came out into the open air that was chill and still dark with only the edges of the eastern horizon light-ening, she hesitated with her hand on the car door as for some inexplicable reason her words of the previous even-ing clicked into her mind like a needle slotting into the groove of a record. 'But knowing I wasn't a coward. . . .'

'And yet, if anything,' she whispered to herself as a

playful dawn breeze blew her hair across her face, 'of all the acts of cowardice I've committed surely this has to be the worst? I mean, he's proved beyond doubt that he's a deeply sensitive, committed man in so many ways. He cares about people, he cares about the environment. And it's true, I did have to go to extraordinary lengths last night. . . .'

And yet here I am still running away. I've learnt nothing of value. Only that I *am* a coward.

The morning air was fresh on her skin—so fresh she shivered suddenly. Then she straightened and dropped her hand from the car door, breathing deeply as if she was welcoming the invigorating coolness around her. And without giving herself time to think again she went back in through the green front door and climbed the stairs.

Steve was still standing in the middle of the room as if he hadn't moved since she left.

She stopped a few paces from him and said haltingly, 'I was wrong. I've been wrong all the way through. It *is* wrong not to give something a chance to . . . well. . . .' She shrugged and clenched her fists in an agony of uncertainty as she searched his face for some kind of response but found none.

'What I mean is,' she swallowed and then said in a rush, 'if you still want me I'll be your . . . your. . . .'

'Mistress?' he supplied the single word coolly.

She bit her lip. 'Yes. If you still want me,' she added barely audibly and unable to meet his eye.

The silence stretched. Oh God! she thought, he's going to knock me back now.

But when he spoke it was to say in the same cool voice, 'Provided I can call the tune. Change the conditions slightly.'

She lifted her head then to stare at him with wide, wary eyes. 'How do you mean?' she asked huskily.

'I mean, Morgan, that if I make you my mistress, I also make you my wife and ultimately the mother of my children. *Our* children. Because, you see, I'm afraid the contract is unacceptable to me any other way.'

She couldn't believe she'd heard him right. 'You want to marry me?' she said incredulously.

He stepped forward so that he was within reach of her, but he didn't touch her. 'I want to marry you, Morgan,' he said sombrely. 'I want to be your husband, your lover, your teacher and your pupil.'

'What could I ever teach you?' she murmured dazedly, and trembled as he reached out a hand to loop her hair through his fingers and then let his hand lie at the base of her throat.

'More than you'll ever know, Morgan,' he said, his lips barely moving and his lids half lowered over the blue blue of his eyes. 'Only last night you gave me a lesson in gallantry I'll never forget. I've never made love to any woman before who gave herself so completely as you did. There's an old saying about virgins, but you re-wrote the book last night, Morgan. Did I . . . hurt you very much?'

She closed her eyes at the deep caressing note in his voice and wondered wildly if she was imagining all this.

'So what's it to be?' he asked as his other hand came up to slip beneath her blouse and lie on her shoulder.

'But,' her voice shook, 'you think I'm neurotic and unstable. And. . . .'

'No,' he interjected, 'I said those things to jolt you. I knew what kind of turmoil you were going through. But they say all's fair in love and war, and I was fighting for my very life. I have been for months.'

'You didn't say. . . .'

'Only because I knew you'd basically mistrust a declaration of love. I knew it was something you didn't understand—through no real fault of your own—that it was something tarnished and unreal to you. But occasionally, despite my good intentions, I got carried away.'

He let his eyes roam broodingly from her lips to where her button was straining across her breasts above his wandering fingers.

'Not without provocation either,' he added as that muscle moved in his jaw. 'Just the look of you is enough provocation to me, my dear. But when you increase it with everything else I love about you—your intelligence, your stubbornness, your humanity—well, it got too much for me on occasions.'

'*My* humanity?' she queried wonderingly.

'Yes,' he replied, and released her hair to draw her forward so that her forehead rested on his shoulder. 'If you knew the gauntlet of concerned neighbours I had to run, when you came out of hospital!'

'But. . . .'

'But nothing, Morgan,' he said quietly. 'They all love you because they value you.'

'Oh, Steve,' she said tearfully, 'I've done so little really.'

He tilted her chin upwards. 'It seems that way because it's second nature to you.'

'But last night. . . .' she said hesitantly. 'You were so cold.' She shivered as she recalled the crystal glass flashing through the air reflecting the firelight brilliantly before it disappeared into the darkness of the night.

'Last night,' he murmured against her throat, 'was the only time I gave up hope. That picture in the paper . . . you know, you asked me about Leonie? It was ironic really, because up until last night, although I'd written it, I hadn't really believed it was possible to be spurred to an act of violence because of what you felt for someone. And yet I could have gone out and killed that man!'

'Oh, Steve,' she said again, and felt a deep tremor at the pit of her stomach as his roving fingers found and plucked gently at her nipple.

'I like the way you say that. Why don't you say it again? You know, in nearly,' he shrugged, 'six months you've hardly ever called me by my name. Until last night, that is,' he amended. 'And then you said it with every shade of meaning of your voice—and your body.'

'I . . . I . . . Oh! Why . . . what are you doing?' she asked painfully as he released her.

'Because I meant what I said.' He turned his back to her on a suddenly rough note. 'I need you. I need you in a thousand ways—slim and lissom as you are now but also burgeoning with child, vulnerable as you've never been and *my* responsibility. But I couldn't do it unless it was a total commitment.'

He swung round to face her suddenly. 'Those are my terms,' he said unevenly. 'What are yours?'

'My terms?' she said slowly. 'I don't have any. But I do want to say something. Last night, for the first time in my life, I felt like a woman. Like the women you told me about—those who lived by instinct. Only I felt even above and beyond them. Because it was you. I felt enriched beyond compare, because it was your bed. And . . . I understood what you meant when you talked about the key to men's hearts and what Ryan meant when he talked about . . . if you couldn't lie down with joy you shouldn't lie down at all. I knew it all for a basic truth. Knew it academically—but also only because it was you.' She plaited her fingers. 'I could never have done it for any other man. I . . . oh, Steve. . . .'

'Say it,' he murmured as his arms reached for her. 'I must warn you, I'll never tire of hearing it.'

'Oh, Steve, I love you. But then I always did.'

'And I love you, Morgan my darling.'

'Yes,' Ryan said warily into the phone. 'Yes, it's me, Mr Harrow. How . . . how are you?' he added tentatively. His expression lightened somewhat. 'Good! What's that? Can I cope on my own for the day? Sure! Do you mean Morgan's not coming in? Is she all right? You're getting *married*!'

His voice cracked on a high note and drew the attention of a thin elderly lady who wandered over to his desk and waved a brochure at him.

'Hang on,' Ryan said into the phone, his eyes still bulging visibly. 'Won't you sit down, madam,' he said to the lady. 'I shan't be a minute, but the most amazing thing has happened!'

He turned back to the phone. 'When?' he said eagerly. 'Tomorrow? That's great, but hang on. Who's going to give her away? Because I reckon I've earned that task, mate!'

He put the phone down a few minutes later and beamed joyfully at his client. 'They're getting married tomorrow,' he said confidentially to her. 'Mind you, if you ask me, I'd have done it yesterday. She can be mighty hard to pin down, still. . . .' He broke off and smacked his head playfully. 'I wonder where they're going on their honeymoon? I really should have recommended Fiji or Pago Pago.'

The lady stared at him with her lips slightly parted.

'You do realise,' Ryan said earnestly to her, 'what this means, don't you? In effect, it could mean I'll be planning my own honeymoon some day soon. When she's got over it, that is . . . perhaps somewhere more peaceful would be better. As a woman of the world, madam, wouldn't you agree you need peace and quiet on your honeymoon? After all. . . .'

The lady rose with very careful movements. '*You* need peace and quiet, sonny,' she said sternly. 'You need a straitjacket!'

'I? said Ryan, rising too and seemingly quite oblivious to the ripple of interest he was creating along the length and breadth of the agency which even caused the manager's head to poke alarmingly from his cloistered cubicle.

'I?' said Ryan again in ringing tones as the lady backed towards the door. 'Believe me, madam, I deserve a medal! If it wasn't for me. . . .'

THE BEAUTY OF ADONIS

Most people know that the change of the seasons is caused by the rotation of the earth on its axis. But thousands of years ago the people of ancient Greece had a much more colorful explanation. They believed that the transformation from summer to winter was the result of the rivalry between two goddesses for the love of the beautiful youth Adonis.

According to the myth, Adonis was conceived by Myrrh, whose father, angered by his daughter's pregnancy, threatened to kill her. To save Myrrh, the gods turned her into a tree, which bears her name. After ten months a wild boar gouged the tree with its horn and from within came the baby Adonis. Aphrodite, the goddess of love, was smitten with his extraordinary beauty. She put the infant into a chest, and for safekeeping gave him to Persephone, queen of the netherworld and goddess of the dead. Persephone's curiosity overwhelmed her, and she peeked into the chest. She, too, became so entranced by Adonis's beauty that she refused to give him back to Aphrodite. To settle the problem, Zeus, the king of the gods, decreed that Adonis should spend half of every year with Aphrodite, and the other half with Persephone.

Thus Adonis's yearly visit to the netherworld became the time of winter, and his return to Aphrodite marked the beginning of spring and a new summer.

Today, it is sometimes tempting to call a very handsome man an Adonis. Yet how could any mortal quite match the beauty of one whose looks inspired a legend that has existed for thousands of years!

HELP HARLEQUIN PICK 1982's GREATEST ROMANCE!

We're taking a poll to find the most romantic couple (real, not fictional) of 1982. Vote for any one you like, but please vote and mail in your ballot today. As Harlequin readers, you're the real romance experts!

Here's a list of suggestions to get you started. Circle your choice, or print the names of the couple you think is the most romantic in the space below.

Prince of Wales / Princess of Wales

Luke / Laura (General Hospital stars)

Gilda Radner / Gene Wilder

Jacqueline Bisset / Alexander Godunov

Mark Harmon / Christina Raines

Carly Simon / Al Corley

Susan Seaforth / Bill Hayes

Burt Bacharach / Carole Bayer Sager

_____
(please print)
_____

_____

Please mail to: Maureen Campbell
Harlequin Books
225 Duncan Mill Road
Don Mills, Ontario, Canada
M3B 3K9